DESTINY

Nadine A. Goins

Copyright 2020 by Nadine Goins

www.born2dream.com

Cover design by The Ezer Agency

Editing Services: Riel Felice

Formatting Services: Darío de los Santos

ISBN: 1732411522, 9781732411524

Contents

Acknowledgements

To my first born son:

I never thought that I could love someone more than I loved myself, but every day since February 27, 2013, you have shown me that there is more to life than just wealth.

I promise to do everything in my power to provide the best life for you and be the best mother that I can be.

On those days that I feel like giving up, I take one glance at your sweet face, and then I realize that you're the reason that I breathe.

There is nothing that you can do to make me stop loving you; because my love is unconditional and my loyalty remains true

I will always be by your side. No matter what, your Grandma and I are always down to ride (lol!).

I love you more than life itself. No fame, no riches, no wealth;

God blessed me with the greatest gift that I may ever know— and that's being your mother and watching you grow!

Love Mom

Dedication

This book is dedicated to the women who first inspired me: Whitney Houston, Nadine W., Juneza R., Naomi L., Elnoria P., Georgia (Madea) W., and Angela H. You all have paved the way for me; you gave me wings so that I may be free to soar far beyond the sky with limitless boundaries.

To my loving daddy, my hero, my heart in human form, Darrin Reasby. You gave me a sense of hope to persevere through anything in life. Your strength through your heart transplant shows me the power of God at its finest. Thank you for your guidance, inspiration, and motivation on those days when I felt like my dreams could not be attained. Your wisdom and tender care is what every girl needs from her daddy. Thanks for always only being a phone call away and a shoulder to cry on. I will never forget the memories that we've shared. You'll always be my hero! I love you and I'm proud to say that I will always be a daddy's girl deep down inside. Rest in peace, daddy.

To my sonshine, Joseph A. III: You gave me purpose in life. Thank you for loving me in the midst of it all; I promise to leave a legacy for you to follow for decades to come.

Last, but certainly not least, my papa, Elbridge John Lock, as well as A.L. Goins: I miss you every second of every day that passes by. My life has never been the same since the day you physically left, but I know that you all are smiling down on me. I pray that I made you both proud!

I love you all for life and long after life ends. THANK YOU for your contributions to my life. Some things money can't buy, and for that alone, I am grateful.

A Letter To My Daddy

How do I say goodbye to my best friend?

The tears I cry are only a reflection of the leaking hole in my heart that will never mend.

You're the only person that has never told me no and at my lowest moment in life, you gave me hope.

When it came to this thing called life, you showed me the ropes.

You never let distance get in the way of being present in my life for every milestone, just to show me how much you cared.

I promise to always cherish the memories that we've shared.

I never had to wonder if I was loved by anyone because I've always had you.

It's a cold world we live in, what's a daddy's girl to do?

But I'll hold my head up high and carry on as I replay the moments when you reminded me that I am strong.

So don't you fret and don't you dare cry, for this is a transition to a new beginning and new beginnings never start with goodbye…

I'll love you forever, daddy.

Love Always,

The Woman

CHAPTER 1

Dear Life,

As I sit here starting into the sky watching the waves pass me by, I wonder where we will end up. Where will you take me? What will I see? Sometimes I wonder if happiness is meant to be, and most of all, if it is meant for me. I'm tired of the hurt, anger, and lies that come with life. I'm tired of the pain, loneliness, and unheard cries. Sometimes, I go to sleep and hope that my eyes won't open the next day. It's at times like these that I'm at a loss for words and don't know what to say. How many more times will I cry before I begin to smile? Sometimes I want to pack my bags, or pack nothing at all, and disappear for a while. Life is too short to not enjoy it while I still have it, but why is mine filled with such misery and havoc? Looking from the outside in, everything looks perfect and destiny is bound to win. But if you take a closer look, you'll see that there lies a girl who feels alone and misunderstood, without family or even one true friend. No one can take away this gift God gave me. God's love for me is one thing I'm sure will never go astray. Maybe happiness will find me one day, but destiny is something that will forever stay…

My name is Destiny Alexander. The world was blessed with my presence on July 7, 1990. I am the oldest of my mother's two children; my brother Anthony is two years younger than me. Life hasn't always been easy being raised by a single mother. My parents separated after my first birthday and Anthony never knew his real father. We were raised in a two-bedroom apartment in the heart of Memphis, Tennessee. With the stress of working three jobs to support two children, my mom never really had time to spend with us. Sometimes, we were subject to the backlash of all of the stress she dealt with. Occasionally, she used cocaine and would beat me and Anthony with whatever object she was closest to. Most of the time, I would shield Anthony from the blows. He was younger than me, so I knew that he couldn't handle the distress as well as I could. Anthony and I shared the same room, so we had a lot of time to spend together. We promised that we would never abandon one another.

After graduating high school in the top ten percent of my class, I was eligible for a full scholarship to the University of North Texas at Dallas. I could finally escape the horror of the ghetto and the abuse, a decision that Anthony would never forgive me for. After I left for college, Anthony was left to the streets to provide for himself; this is something he has always resented me for. I always promised him that once he graduated high school, I would get a place in Dallas and send for him to come stay with me.

My mother didn't show up to my high school graduation. In fact, she didn't give a damn about anyone else besides herself by the time we were teenagers. By then, she had lost two of her jobs and was left to depend on welfare for the core of her survival; she began to use cocaine more heavily and became more distant from her family. When the time came for me to leave for college, I was left with the money I had received from my home church as a love gift for graduation. I was forced to use a portion of it to buy a one way bus ticket to Dallas, Texas to pursue my education.

There I was, standing on the curb waiting for my taxi with my two bags and my 16-year-old little brother who hated to see me go. Tears fell from my eyes as I faced the one fear I never wanted to become reality: me leaving Anthony alone.

"I will always love you, Ant. I promise to send for you when you graduate," I said, crying as I hugged him.

"I know you do, sis. Go get your degree, you deserve it. I'mma come visit you in the D-town. I love you more than anything in this world," Anthony said while fighting his tears. He eventually lost the battle once he saw the taxi pulling up to the curb.

"This isn't goodbye, Anthony," I promised while putting my things in the taxi.

"I know, sis. I'm gonna miss you. Call me when you make it to Dallas," he urged while hugging me tightly for the last time.

"Where to?" the taxi driver asked.

"Greyhound bus station on Airways Boulevard," I sniffled through my tears.

I couldn't help but look out of the back window as we drove away from my past life, only to see Anthony still standing on the curb watching me leave. His face was filled with disappointment.

CHAPTER 2

Untouchable

It's like being in the sky and you can't reach the stars.

It's like having the world in your hands and you can't reach Mars.

As I stare at the reflection in the mirror trying to reach deep down in my soul, searching for the bottom of the never-ending hole.

It's like receiving a million dollar postdated check, recalling the ups and downs that left my life a wreck.

It's like reaching the end of eternity.

It's like being released from jail but never truly being set free.

My love for you is untouchable; it can't be reached.

Kinda like reading a book on life, preparing for a lesson you can never teach.

It's like waiting until the end of forever.

Will your love return? Never say never.

Motivation

Life is like a movie that will never rewind.

Stay tuned and press play and watch your destiny unwind.

So many people press pause and focus in on the old me.

It's too bad that they never press play and get to know who I'm destined to be.

Still striving to be the best, never stopping to settle for anything less.

So many people stay stuck in the past, till holding onto memories and hoping those moments will last.

It's the future that holds the most weight.

When your future is as bright as the sun, it's the future that the haters love to hate.

So to my haters, I'll spare you the humiliation. Getting my education is my only motivation.

I'm driven by determination. Where do we go when this world we live in is filled with desperation?

Bound by limitless segregation, swallowed by deprivation, still facing discrimination, we must discover that there is no limitation.

After the nine-hour bus ride, I finally arrived at my dorm on campus. The University of Village is what they called it. As I began to take my things out of the taxi, I began to get nervous with the thought of not knowing what my journey as a college freshman had in store for me. It was refreshing to smell the fresh air, hear the sound of traffic moving along, and see parents smiling and laughing while helping their children move into the dorm. It was something I wished that I, too, could have. There I stood, all alone—at five feet, six inches tall, with my mocha chocolate complexion; bone-straight hair that reached my shoulders; and a small figure—with my blue jeans and my pink Hollister t-shirt, ready to take on the world.

After unloading my things from the taxi, I swiftly approached the double doors to the entrance of my dorm. By the time I reached the front desk after maneuvering my way through the crowd of movers, I came into contact with Mrs. Jones, one of the assistants who was helping to check everyone in. She was an older, short, yellow-toned woman with short, red hair and a heavyset figure.

"Hi! Welcome to your new beginning as a college student. My name is Mrs. Jones. How may I help you today?" exclaimed Mrs. Jones over the noisy crowd.

"Hey, Mrs. Jones. I'm Destiny Alexander and I need to get my key to my room."

"Okay, sweetie. Let me get you to fill out these housing forms. Do you have your ID?"

"Yes, ma'am, I do," I stated after reaching into my purse and taking out my Memphis identification card. Mom never had a car for me, so I couldn't take the road test and get my driver's license.

"Alright. Now that you have completed your forms, here is your key to suite 107, room A. It's right around this corner to the left," she said, pointing me in the direction of my new home.

"Okay, thank you!" I said as I gathered my bags and headed to my room. The hallway was well-lit and there was a camera on every corner of the dingy yellow walls. The carpet was dark red and in desperate need of a good steam cleaning treatment. Finally, I had arrived at my room. I stood in front of a tall wooden door with a small peephole in the center. As the door crept open, I saw three rooms, each with a small frame wooden door. I was simultaneously greeted by the smell of bleach and Pine-Sol—at that moment,I noticed that the bathroom and the sink to my right had already been wiped down. I then heard a door open before I could even put my bags in my room. There stood a smiling girl at five foot, three inches, with a slender frame, big light brown eyes, a light complexion, and sandy brown hair that reached past the middle of her back.

"Hey, roomie! I'm Christine. Nice to meet you!" the overjoyed girl exclaimed while extending her hand out for a handshake. Christine was a mulatto, raised as an only child by her married, wealthy parents in Houston, Texas. She was spoiled her entire life and didn't know what it was like not to be celebrated for her accomplishments and birthdays. She drove a black 2008 Mercedes Benz and her room was decked out with pictures of her family and friends; colorful pink sheets; designer bags; a closet full of clothes and shoes; a miniature fridge; a microwave; a laptop computer with a printer set up on her desk; and a 32-inch flat screen plasma TV to top it all off. Her parents wanted to make sure that she didn't have any worries while in school, so they stacked her bank account with tons of cash so she wouldn't have to work. She was as sweet as sweet potato pie, but didn't have a speck of common sense in the real world. In the hood, we call kids like her "silver spoon fed." Most of the time, they were subject to being jacked for their nice things.

"Hi, I'm Destiny. Nice to meet you, too." I unenthusiastically stated as I shook her hand.

"Well, our other roommate hasn't gotten here yet, but I'm excited to meet her! I'm from Houston, Texas. Where are you from, Destiny?" she asked.

"I'm from Memphis, Tennessee. Do you know when orientation will be?" I asked, trying to change the subject and take the attention off of myself.

"Yeah, I think it's scheduled for Monday morning at 9:00. So, is your family outside getting the rest of your stuff?"

"Nah, this is all I have. My parents already left," I replied, looking down at the floor. I lied to the cheerful girl, who apparently didn't have a clue that not everyone has a loving family.

"I'm so sorry about that," she sympathetically stated.

"Nah, girl. You good," I reassured.

"Let's put your things in your room. I'll help you. And if you need anything, I'm right next to you in room B," she stated as she grabbed one of my two bags.

"Gee, thanks, Christine! That's really sweet of you."

"Well, you know, I try to be nowadays," Christine stated as we giggled in unison. Silence fell upon the room for a split second before we heard the doorknob turn and the door open. In walked a brown-skinned girl who stood at five feet, five inches tall and had chin-length jet black hair. Nicole was what we called a thick girl; she had the big, gigantic booty that men loved and mid-sized, full breasts. She was followed by a tall, dark-skinned guy with a nappy afro and a heavyset woman with a caramel complexion and a short red and black quick weave. They were there to assistNicole move her things into the dorm.

Nicole was raised by her mom in Arlington, Texas. Nicole's mother separated from her father before she was born, but he typically was in the picture for the important events in her life, such as some birthdays and most graduations. At least she had more than what I had in a father. She had five brothers and sisters, so she never knew what it was like to feel special, even though she already knew that she was. Seeing that she was the youngest daughter and the fourth-born child, she was the first out of her siblings to further her education after high school. Her oldest sister, Monique, already had three children at the age of 26; Tashara had one baby girl; and Mike, her oldest brother, dropped out of high school by the 11th grade, which led to him becoming a notorious criminal before the age of 18. As for the rest of her siblings, Bruce graduated on time from high school and was now a manager at the local McDonald's, whereas Brandon had one more year of high school before graduation.

"Heeeey, ladies! I'm Nicole. Nice to meet you!" she smiled as she extended her hand for a handshake.

"Hello, Nicole! I'm Christine! It's a pleasure to meet you, as well!" exclaimed Christine as she returned the gesture.

"Nice to meet you, Nicole. I'm Destiny," I said, smiling as I shook her hand.

"And these are my parents, Jonathan and Tamra," she introduced us to her parents as they sat her things down to shake our hands. After the introduction, three boys and two girls carried Nicole's belongings into the suite.

"And these are my brothers and sisters. This is Monique, Tashara, Mike, Bruce, and Brandon," she said, introducing her siblings as they all said "Hey" in unison.

"Hey, everyone! Nice to meet you all," Christine and I responded. Nicole's sisters resembled her body type—they were thick in frame with similar complexions. Monique was a little chubbier than the rest, with two-toned gold and black microbraids. Tashara seemed a tad bit more reserved, with full breasts, a huge booty, and a natural afro. Mike was tall and appeared to be the oldest out of the bunch; he was all muscle with dreads and gold teeth. Bruce was brown-skinned, short, and fat with braids, while Brandon seemed to be the most opposite of them all with his slender physique, caramel skin, and low haircut.

"Okay, well, I will let you guys get back to moving in, and maybe we can all hang out sometime," Christine stated as she slowly exited my room.

"Oh, yeah, girl! That sounds like fun!" exclaimed Nicole.

"Okay, cool. Sounds like a plan," I responded.

Nicole and the crew went back to moving her in as I settled into my room. After hearing the door close and seeing my room, with its four walls and a window, I finally realized that I was all alone in Dallas, Texas. I was going after what no one else in my family had ever dared to obtain—a degree. After unpacking my clothes, I placed my sheets on my twin bed and cleaned my room. I didn't have much, but I knew from that moment forward that I would strive to make a better life for myself and my family.

CHAPTER 3

No Name

Handsome, intelligent, swag just right; his vibe is so serene.

This kind of man is only fit for a queen.

If only I knew your name, my personal celebrity, no fame.

I find myself falling for you, Mr. Anonymous.

This kind of attraction goes far beyond lust; I look forward to seeing your face every day.

I love everything about you in every way.

If I had the chance, I'd treat you like a king;

I'd cater to you and give you everything.

You're more than just a handsome face.

You're the perfect gentleman with dignity and grace.

I need you in every way; I breathe you in with every breath I take.

My love for you is deeper than any ocean, sea, or lake.

My personal celebrity, no fame, I've fallen for you and I don't even know your name.

Man of My Dreams

Gentle, thoughtful, and everything that love may seem,

God created you to be the man of my dreams.

You're on my mind every second of the day; my body yearns for you in every way.

You leave me speechless, what more can a girl say?

If patience is a virtue, you're worth the wait. For you, I'll wait forever and a day.

If I had the chance, I'd make you mine.

Seal it, stamp it, and sign my name on the dotted line.

This feeling we share makes everything complete; I will never stray away because we're meant to be.

Everything may not always be what they seem, but I do believe that I just met the man of my dreams.

Perfect Guy

I wish that I could create the perfect guy: handsome, smart, serene, and not too shy.

He would meet all of his woman's needs, and when she talks, he wouldn't just listen; he would take heed because he understands that HE can be all that she needs.

He would fill her day with smiles in each and every way, and when she cries on his shoulder, he would always know just what to say.

He would hold her in his arms each and every night, and when the sun rises, he'd let her know that she's the sunshine that makes his day bright.

I wish that I could create the perfect guy: strong but gentle. He doesn't have to wear a suit and a tie.

He would tell her the truth and never harm her with lies.

He would never abandon her with unsaid goodbyes.

He would hug and kiss her just to let her know that he still cares.

He'll show her every day that he appreciates the love that they share.

I wish that I could create the perfect guy: thoughtful and understanding, but not too shy. Maybe then we could begin with just a simple Hi.

As I opened my eyes, I took a look outside to see that the sun was shining and the birds were chirping. The day couldn't be more perfect—it was my first day at freshman orientation. As I made my way to the bathroom to shower and prepare for my day, I saw Christine and Nicole getting ready at the sink for our big day.

"Good morning, girls!" I greeted the ladies before entering the bathroom.

"Hey, girl!" Nicole responded.

"Good morning, Destiny!" Christine joyfully stated.

"Does anybody know what time freshman orientation starts?" I asked.

"Um, yeah, I think it starts at 10. I think we all should go together, if you guys are cool with that," Christine suggested.

"Yeah, girl! That's fine. Let me hurry up and get dressed," I agreed.

"Ooh, yeah, girl! That's what's up. I was thinking the same thang! I haven't met any new friends out here on campus yet, so I think we should stick together, you know?" explained Nicole.

"Okay, cool," we agreed.

After getting dressed, we walked to the gymnasium where the core of the orientation was held. There were tons of students scattered everywhere from wall to wall. My heart began pounding faster, like it always does when I get nervous. Before walking into the auditorium, I noticed a tall, handsome guy with caramel skin and a fresh haircut flooded with waves. He was neatly dressed in a collared polo with jeans and Sperrys, standing against the wall and conversing with his two buddies who looked like basketball players. We immediately made eye contact and engaged in a r gaze that seemed to last forever. He slowly approached me and introduced himself while his friends introduced themselves to

Christine and Nicole and began a conversation off to the side.

"Well, hello, beautiful. I'm John, but my friends and family call me Jay. What's your name?" he asked.

"Hey, Jay. My name is Destiny. Nice to meet you. You are extremely tall," I stated jokingly.

"Yeah, I play basketball. Where are you from?" he smiled.

"Oh, okay! You're an athlete. That explains it! I'm from Memphis, Tennessee. Where are you from?"

"Aww, okay. I've never been to Tennessee; I'm from St. Louis, Missouri. So, did you leave a boyfriend back in Tennessee?" he curiously asked.

I laughed. "Actually, I sure didn't! Did you leave a girl crying when you left Missouri?"

"Nope, not at all. I prefer to leave them smiling! But I'm single, and if it's alright with you, can we exchange numbers so that I can get to know you better?"

"Yeah , I think we can make that happen," I responded while taking out my cell phone to plug his number in.

Just as I was in the middle of giving him my number, there was an announcement made for all of the students to enter the auditorium for orientation to begin. Christine and Nicole seemed to be on the same page with the guys they spoke to as we all gathered together to find a seat for the two-hour freshman class presentation.

Following the orientation, we walked back to the dorm while discussing the guys we had just met. Christine and Nicole both seemed highly intrigued by the guys and had high hopes of dating them.

"So, Destiny, what did you think of that fine ass nigga you was talking to?" Nicole asked.

I laughed. "Girl! He was fine, huh?! His name is Jay and he plays basketball. We exchanged numbers, so I guess I'll be hearing from him soon."

"Yeah, his friends that we were talking to play basketball, too. The guy I met, his name was Adrian. I like him already and I gave him my number, so maybe he'll hit me up," Christine added.

"Hell yeah, Christine! He was fine as hell, too!" Nicole interrupted.

"The nigga I was talking to, his name was Chris. Now he can get it fa'sho! Y'all already know I gave him my number! We're supposed to meet up later, but there's a party happening tonight, so I might just wait and see him afterwards. Y'all down with going to the party tonight?"

"Hell, yeah! I wanna go! Who gon' drive, though? 'Cuz we ain't got no car." I replied.

"Girl, I got a car! I'll drive! We gon' have a good time tonight, and it's gon' be our first night out as college freshmen! I'm too geeked," Christine explained.

"Aww, hell yeah! Dat's what's up, Christine! You not as stuck-up as I thought you'd be! So, what kinda car you got?" Nicole asked.

Christine laughed. "Well, damn! Thanks, I think! Y'all about to see it right now. It's right over there in the corner next to that red Honda," she said while pointing in the direction of a black Mercedes Benz as we approached the parking lot of our dorm. Our mouths dropped as we headed towards the luxury car in amazement.

"Girl, I know damn well yo' parents ain't buy you a Benz! Y'all must be balling!" Nicole shouted in excitement.

Christine smiled. "Yeah, my parents do alright financially. Plus, I'm the only kid they have, anyway."

"Damn, girl, this car is nice as hell! We finna be stuntin' on they asses tonight!" I exclaimed.

"Hell, yeah! We finna be stuntin'. Ain't no other damn freshmen riding in a Benz! Christine, you lucky as fuck. I wish I had wealthy parents like yours! Hell, I wish I was the only damn child, at least! All the brothers and sisters I got I ain't never really had a lot of new stuff 'cuz my shit be hand-me-downs from everybody else before me," Nicole explained while looking into the sky as if she could really see herself in Christine's shoes.

"Yeah, girl, you lucky as hell! I just wish I had parents who gave a damn enough about me to help me do anything! Instead, I always end up doing shit by myself or with my brother Anthony," I added.

"Wow, Destiny. Is that why you didn't have anybody with you when you moved into the dorm?" Christine asked.

Looking down at the ground, I responded with shame. "Yeah, that's right. My mom has a lot going on right now and my dad hasn't been in my life since I was one year old. Maybe one day I will fill you guys in on the details of my horrible life, but for now, let's just have a good time."

"Damn, girl, that's fucked up. I'm here if you ever wanna talk.

Don't trip; my life wasn't peaches and cream, either, with all the damn brothers and sisters I've got!" Nicole added in hopes of making me feel better.

"Aww, Destiny, I'm so sorry to hear that. I will always be here for you whenever you need me. Somehow, I feel like I've known you guys forever, but I think we will build a bond that is unbreakable. As long as we stick together, we will make it through anything," Christine reassured me.

Christine's encouraging words seemed to uplift all of us in that moment.

"Gee, thanks, ladies. Yeah, I feel like we have known each other for a while, or at least grew up together. I'm glad to know that I'm not on this journey alone. I will always be here for you skeezas as well!" I laughed.

"Skeeza! Girl, put 'paid' in front of it and you've got yourself a deal!" Nicole jokingly added.

We grabbed a bite to eat at the café and began preparing for our night of fun. Time flew by before it was time to go to the party and we managed to get our hands on vodka and cranberry juice before getting to our destination.

The parking lot was packed and the building appeared to be small. As we entered the party, the musk of body odor and the overbearing scents perfume and cologne collided. The party was packed and the music was blasting; people were bumping and grinding on each other up against the wall and shoulder to shoulder. We quickly joined the crowd and made our way through the party as we danced to the beat of the loud music. Before I knew it, we were all paired up with niggas grinding on our asses like there was no tomorrow.

Two hours passed and we were still going strong at the party before we bumped into Jay, Chris, and Adrian. We immediately grabbed them and gave them a taste of what they would get in the bedroom with us. I was pleased to feel Jay's long, hard erection while grinding on him to a slow jam. That was just the confirmation I needed to know that he was feeling me and my movement and that he had a mandingo dick, something I couldn't wait to feel inside of me.

The party ended at 2:30 in the morning. By then, our hormones were raging and we were ready to pounce on each other. Christine decided to take Adrian with her, leaving Nicole and Chris to venture off alone and me and

Jay to have our alone time.

After arriving in the parking lot of the dorm, we began ripping each other's clothes off. His kiss was soft like a pillow and his body was rock solid, equipped with a six-pack and covered in tattoos. As he gently laid me down in the back seat of his truck, he began slowly kissing my lips and working his way down to my nipples, taking as much of my breasts into his warm, wet mouth as he could. I could feel my panties getting wetter by the second. After teasing me with his tongue, he eventually arrived at the tip of my clitoris as he vibrated his moist tongue up and down, in and out. Grinding my pelvis against the motions of his tongue, I quickly exploded with cum all over his face. Wanting to return the favor, I laid him on his back and gently began teasing the tip of his dick by flicking my tongue, slowly working every bit of his eight-inch penis into my mouth.

He grasped the back of my head and moaned as I deep throated his manhood. Just before he arrived at the peak of his pleasure, I got up and waited for him to put the condom on before climbing on top of him to give him the real deal of my riding skills. He dug around in his wallet, then located the condom and put it on. I began to kiss him as I climbed on top of him. As I thrusted on his long, hard erection, he palmed my breasts and licked them with passion. It wasn't long before he

let out a loud moan, assuring me that he had reached his peak by oozing cum into the condom.

"Damn, boo. You got me sweating," I panted.

"You got me sweating too, baby, but that shit was great!" he laughed.

"Yeah, I enjoyed you, too."

"When can we do this again?" he asked.

"Whenever you think you can handle another session with me," I smiled as I put my clothes back on.

"Shit, I can handle one right now! Well, as soon as I get another erection!" he joked.

"Nah, not right now. I'm tired and ready to go to bed," I explained.

"Okay, that's cool. Have a good night, sweetheart. I'll see ya later," he stated as he kissed me on the lips.

"Okay, goodnight," I responded as I exited his truck to go into the dorm. The walk to the door seemed like an eternity, especially since he was a gentleman and waited for me to enter the door. Damn, I can't believe I just fucked this nigga on the first day I met him, I thought. He probably won't take me seriously now; he probably thinks I'm too easy. I refuse to have any regrets about my decision, so I guess I'll just wait to see how this plays out.

As I entered the corridor of the dorm, it was completely silent and there was no one to be seen except for the receptionist at the front desk. It was now 4:30 a.m. and time had flown by faster than I thought it would. The lights in Nicole's and Christine's rooms were off. I figured they were sleeping—No need to disturb them, I thought. I quickly entered my room, gathered my pajamas, and headed for the shower.

CHAPTER 4

What Lies Within

What lies within a sea of uncertainty?

It's like seeing the shadows of the past and the present. Who knows what the future might be?

I'm constantly torn between my mind and the feelings that lie within me.

How do I handle my battle with hate and envy?

I'm softly treading this path of uncertainty, unlocking the door without the key, still feeling like no one understands me.

What lies within a broken heart?

Someone who left me and left my heart torn apart.

What lies within a broken mind?

Freedom, feelings, and thoughts I may never find.

Between love and hate lies the thin line; it's giving something away that has always been mine.

What truly lies deeply within my soul?

I find myself swimming in emotions that I can't control.

So, what lies within the tenacious being that walks this earth?

A God-fearing woman who knows her worth!

Where to Go

Where do you go when you feel all alone?

Where do you rest your head when you have no place to call home? I wanna know why the caged bird sings.

I wanna know why marriage is symbolized with a ring.

Where would you go if you couldn't read and write?

How do you find peace of mind when you're surrounded by the fuss and the fight?

The little girl who never got the chance to be a daddy's girl—where does she go??

The little boy who doesn't have a father in this world —what does he do?

Where does society leave room for people like us?

Who do you talk to when you don't know who to trust?

What's left to do when you feel like giving up?

What's left to pour when you can't fill an empty cup?

Life is like a boat out in the sea. To sail or to sink is the only philosophy.

How do you cope with death, which seems so far away?

How do you escape the pain when you're faced with it every day?

This thing called life doesn't come with directions. Sometimes, you don't know where to go.

Destination: life or death? Perhaps we'll never know.

Eight months had passed and spring break had quickly arrived. Christine and Adrian began dating and were madly in love. Nicole and Chris fucked often but never decided to seriously date each other, especially since Nicole had other guys she was fucking around with at the same time. Jay and I continued seeing each other on a sex-only basis without commitment. He saw a few other girls from time to time, but he wasn't the only guy I was fucking at the time, either. By then, I had met Donald and was contemplating pursuing a serious relationship with him, something he continued to pester me about. Donald was a great guy, but because I was still fooling around with Jay, I couldn't choose between the two, even though I knew who the better option was.

By the time spring break arrived, Nicole and I didn't have any plans, so Christine invited us to join her back home in Houston for the week. We eagerly accepted the invitation, especially since neither one of us had ever been to Houston, Texas before.

"Girl, I am so glad you invited us to come back home with you! I know we finna kick it!" Nicole exclaimed.

"Yeah! I'm happy you invited us, too, Christine, 'cuz I damn sho' didn't know what I was gon' do," I added.

"Now, y'all know that y'all are more than welcome to come home with me. After all we've been through since August, I would be dead wrong not to invite y'all to my hometown!" Christine assured us.

"Well, you just betta get us there safely on this four-hour trip. Otherwise, there won't be no damn friendship!" Nicole laughed.

"Well, you keep talkin' like dat and yo' ass gon' be walkin'!" Christine shot back.

"I'm goin' to sleep on y'all crazy skeezas. Wake me up when we get there," I interrupted.

The trip seemed to take forever before I woke up to seeing a three-story brick house. There was a huge gate surrounding a large piece of land that was big enough to build four houses on. There were two vehicles parked in the huge circular driveway, a black Escalade truck and a BMW 745i. It was clear that these people were well-off and didn't need any handouts. The backyard was enormous and equipped with a huge pool.

"Okay, ladies, we're here! Destiny, wake ya ass up!"

"Damn, Christine! Yo' house looks like a mansion!" I explained as I sat up in the back seat.

"Hell, yeah! Dis a fuckin' mansion, girl! I ain't neva' seen no shit like dis!" Nicole added.

"Trust me, ladies, it's not a mansion—it's only six bedrooms. Come on, let's get our bags out so I can introduce y'all to my parents. They have been dying to meet y'all!"

"'Only six damn bedrooms' my ass. Christine, that's twice the number of rooms my house has! Bitch, you got life twisted if you ain't grateful to be living this good!" Nicole explained.

"I never said that I wasn't grateful, Nicole. I'm just saying that a mansion would probably have more than six rooms. I love my home," Christine reassured Nicole.

"I think this is a beautiful house and I haven't even been inside yet," I added as we gathered our bags and headed for the front door.

The wooden doors were huge, the kind of doors that a butler or maid would answer. The ceilings in the foyer were high and decorated with a large sparkling chandelier, the floors were made up of a tan marble, and the staircase was covered in white carpet. When we entered the home, I immediately noticed the large slanted staircase that led to the bedrooms located upstairs. We were greeted by her parents: a tall, slender black man with a low haircut and a goatee, and a white woman with long, dark hair, a small frame, and green eyes that stood out more than any of her other features. Both of her parents were dressed in seemingly expensive clothing and were happy to see us. Christine ran into her father's arms and greeted both parents with a warm embrace before introducing us.

"Hey, Daddy! Hey, Mama! I missed you guys. These are my friends and roommates, Destiny and Nicole. Ladies, these are my parents, Derrick and Carol!" Christine introduced us as her parents extended their hands for handshakes.

"Hey, nice to meet you," I said as I greeted them with a handshake.

"I'm so glad to finally meet the wonderful parents of Christine. She's a great friend!" Nicole joyfully explained.

"Thanks, Nicole. I'm glad to know we raised her right," Derrick responded.

"Why don't you girls go on upstairs to settle in and get comfortable? Christine, show them to the guest rooms closest to your room," Carol instructed.

"Yes, ma'am! I sure will!"

Christine directed us into two separate rooms. Each had its own bathroom, as well as large windows which gave a beautiful view of the landscape surrounding the home. This is the life, I thought to myself, wishing that I could have been raised like this. I could still hear my mother's voice as I reminisced on the past while enjoying the view outside of the window.

"I know y'all asses went outside when I went to work after I told you not to!" Mama screamed.

We didn't respond because we knew we were guilty. The only thing we kept trying to figure out was how the hell she knew what we were doing when she went to work. One of our nosey ass neighbors must have snitched on us.

"Yes, ma'am," we responded in unison.

It was a horrific sight to witness mama sniff cocaine up her nose and consistently have multiple men in and out of the small apartment we shared. The more she began using the drug, the more weight she lost due to the loss of her appetite. The sound of Christina's voice caused me to snap out of my daydream as she entered the room.

"Are you enjoying the view?" she asked.

"Yeah, it's beautiful."

"Come here. I'll show you and Nicole my room," she insisted as she showed us which one of the massive rooms was her own.

Christine directed us to the room next to the guest room that Nicole was staying in; the walls were painted purple to match her comforter on her cherrywood sleigh bed. Her window resembled the one in the guest room that I was staying in. Her bathroom was clean and decked out in pink and green everything. She had two enormous closets that were well-organized, separating her winter clothes from summer clothes. Designer bags and shoes lined the upper level of both of her closets. There was a massive hand-painted photo of Christine mounted above the headboard of her bed, along with a 42-inch flat screen TV mounted on the wall adjacent to her bed by the bathroom door. It was clear to us that Christine had everything a girl could ever want in life. If only I could walk in her shoes; I wonder what life would be like.

"This room is gorgeous!" I exclaimed.

"Yeah, girl, this room is banging!" Nicole added.

"Thanks, y'all! Come here; y'all can sit on my bed. Let's have girl talk," Christine suggested as she motioned us to join her. "So, Destiny, what's been up with you and Jay? Or, betta yet, you and Donald? He seems like a good guy.

"Damn, you gettin' right to it, ain't you?" I laughed. "I like Donald, but y'all know I'm still fuckin' Jay. That nigga must have put a dick spell on me, 'cuz I can't seem to leave his ass alone!" I joked.

"Bitch, I know Donald's dick ain't that damn bad that ya ass don't know a good man when you see one!" said Nicole.

"I know ya ass ain't talkin' when you damn near done fucked da whole football team and then some, not to mention a coach or two!" I shot back.

"And so what?! This ain't about me right now! We talkin' about yo' dick dilemma!" Nicole yelled.

"Yeah, well, like I said, I really like Donald and I'm seriously considering a relationship with him. It's something he so badly wants," I explained.

"So, what's the problem, Destiny? I don't understand," Christine asked.

"Girl, it's more complicated than words can explain right now. Everybody's relationships ain't as easy as yours and Adrian's meant-to-be ass life! How are y'all doing? I'm surprised you brought us to Houston and not ya boo!" I asked.

"Nah, it's way too soon for Adrian to be meeting my parents right now. I need to make sure he's the one before I introduce him to my family. I love him, but we're just not there yet," Christine responded.

"Yeah, I feel you, but hell, you've met his parents. Don't you think he's gon' be wondering why the hell you haven't bothered to introduce him to your family?" Nicole asked.

"Well, he can wonder all the hell he wants, but we've already had that discussion. What's going on with you and all the drama in your life?" Christine jokingly asked.

"Where the hell do I begin?!" Nicole laughed. "Of course y'all know me and Chris are still fucking around, but he ain't worth shit, so of course it's nothing serious. I met this guy at the mall last week named Winston, and girl, if he ain't got the biggest dick I've ever seen then I don't know what a big dick looks like! Y'all know I had to test drive that!"

"Yeah, ya ass ought to be an instructor by now with all the test driving you've been doin'," I joked.

"Haha, trick. Not funny!" Nicole scolded.

"Girl, get out ya damn feelings. You know I was just playing with yo' sensitive ass," I responded.

"Yeah, whateva'. You ain't no damn saint, either, ya know! Anyway, like I was saying, I like Winston a lot and he got good conversation. He treats me like a lady. He's not in college, but he works full-time at a factory. I'ma give it a while before I make my verdict on whether he's a good guy or not," Nicole added.

"So, do you think that you would seriously date him as a boyfriend?" Christine asked.

"Um, I'm not really sure yet. Right now, I'm just having my fun with him. I guess we'll see what happens later on down the line. I don't like to make assumptions about a guy too soon, 'cuz I could be wrong, of course." Nicole shrugged.

"Well, I know I damn sho' won't be dating Jay's cheating ass! Girl, do you know that I found out that he had a girlfriend back in Missouri a week after we started fucking around? And he got the nerve to think that he's the only one I should be fuckin' with," I added.

"What kind of shit is that?!" Nicole yelled.

"He is a low-down dirty dog with some damn nerve!" Christine responded.

"Yeah, tell me about it. But I've been doing my thang with Donald, anyway, so Jay gon' get kicked to the curb real soon. I deserve better than what he's been doing, and I have a class with one of the skeezas he's screwing!"

"Damn, girl! How you know that? Christine asked.

"It's obvious! He walks her to class every week and kisses her before he leaves, that's how the hell I know!

"Damn, that's fucked up," Nicole added.

"It hurts to have to witness that, especially knowing that I'm still having sex with him, but life goes on. It's not like we're in a relationship," I stated with disappointment.

"Yeah, dat's true, but you still deserve respect to some degree. That's why Chris knows not to do no silly shit like that in front of me—he knows I'll act a fool on his ass! I don't give a damn that we ain't in no relationship. He can do his dirt behind my back, but damn sho' not in my face! I'm just saying," Nicole exclaimed.

"Yeah, but Nicole, she can't control what dat asshole does out in public. Dogs are gonna be dogs in public and in private, so it doesn't matter. Destiny, I feel for you. Girl, you really gotta let his ass go and just be happy with Donald," Christine explained.

"Donald makes me happy and is everything I could ask for in a guy. He deserves someone that'll treat him right. I'm gonna end my affair with Jay and pursue a relationship with Donald."

"That's ya best bet, girlfriend, cuz Jay is low-down," Nicole advised.

"Nicole, since when did you become the Dr. Phil of the crew with all of the drama you have going on?" I laughed.

"Well, it looks like yo' ass needs more than Dr. Phil to fix ya problematic ass life!" she added.

"Both of y'all skeezas got serious mental problems!" Christine joked.

"Chrissy, shut yo' mulatto ass up! Don't act like ya life is so perfect with Adrian and his small-dick-having ass!" Nicole responded.

"How the hell would you know, anyway?" Christine asked, no longer laughing at the comment.

"Don't worry about all that! I was joking, anyway. You must be guilty," Nicole added.

"Both of y'all shut up before something starts that was never intended to happen. Y'all know how y'all can get!" I interrupted.

"Yeah, Chrissy, get the stick out ya ass!" Nicole added.

"Shut up, heffa!" Christine shot back.

Silence fell in the room for a split second before Christine attempted to change the subject and lighten the mood. She asked me how my family was doing.

"They are doing okay, I guess.. I don't hear from my mom too often and Anthony calls me on a weekly basis to check on me," I responded.

"So, your mom doesn't make time for you at all, even though you're down here without family support?" Christine asked in disbelief.

"Yeah. Every now and then, she checks on me, but she has been on drugs for a while now. That led to me and my brother being abused as kids, so we don't have a close relationship with my mom," I responded as unannounced tears began falling down my face.

"Destiny, I am so sorry to hear that. I wish there was something I could do to make it better. I hope you never have to go through that again. I will always be here for you no matter what," Christine assured me as she hugged me tightly.

"You will always have me, too, Destiny. I promise. Don't cry, girl, it's gon' be alright. At least you're in college doing something with yourself to make a better life for yourself and your brother," Nicole added as she joined us in a group hug.

"Thanks, ladies. I truly appreciate it. My life hasn't always been easy; that's why I keep everything bottled up inside of me. I have never really had anyone to confide in other than Anthony. I'm trying to stay optimistic that things will get better with my family, but it gets hard sometimes, especially when I don't hear from any of our other relatives who live in Tennessee. I've felt alone for so long that I seem to have gotten used to it. Ever since my dad left my life after my first birthday and never looked back, I have not felt like I have a reliable parent to depend on . The only thing that I have to remember my father by is a picture of us when I was a child," I sniffled.

"Girl, don't worry about him. He will wish that he was a part of ya life once you become successful and make something of yourself," Christine encouraged.

"Yeah, I wouldn't stress about him, either. That sucks that he doesn't want to be a part of your life, but in the end, you will become a better person because of your situation," Nicole added.

"Gee, thanks, y'all. That means everything to me. I pray that it will all work itself out; that's why I strive to become a better person every day."

"You are already a better person, sweetie. You have made a decision to do something that no one in your family has dared to do: go to college and educate yourself to earn a degree," Christine said.

"Yeah, I know. I refuse to repeat the cycle of what my family has done.

"Keep ya head up, Destiny. We will get through this," Nicole encouraged.

Time flew by as the girls and I discussed our lives. The conversation unexpectedly took a turn when Nicole revealed that during her childhood and early teens, she was raped and consistently sexually abused by a close relative. Before I knew it, we were all in a huddle crying crocodile tears together.

Later that night, Christine's parents took us to dinner at an exquisite restaurant. Nicole and I were amazed at the VIP treatment that we received at the restaurant; the food was the best that I had ever eaten at a restaurant. Her parents asked us how school was going and how our families were doing. We remained respectful while answering her parent's nosy questions, especially the ones about our personal relationships with guys.

Dinner was finally over and we headed back to Christine's home to get ready for bed and prepare for our week of fun. We had lots of activities planned, including horseback riding, shopping, and going to theme parks.

Our week in Houston ended too soon, but we had to return to school to finish our spring semester. Nicole and I didn't want to leave; we enjoyed being apart of Christine's lovely life for a week. If only she could trade places with us for a week—I'm sure she would have a newfound respect for her silver spoon lifestyle. Before loading our bags into the car, we said our goodbyes to her parents and let them know how grateful we were that they welcomed us into their home.

"Thank you, Mr. Derrick and Mrs. Carol, for allowing us into your beautiful home. This was the best spring break that I have ever had!" I joyfully expressed.

"Yeah, we had a great time here in Houston! Thank you both so much for treating us like family and making us feel welcomed," Nicole added.

"You girls are welcome here anytime! We were glad to have you," Derrick stated.

"I'm so glad that you girls decided to spend your break with us. I'm so happy that Christine has found such wonderful friends," Carol explained.

Christine smiled as she hugged her parents and prepared to leave. Her father helped us with our luggage as her mother stood on the front lawn watching us leave.

CHAPTER 5

Dream to Reality

Here we stand face to face.

Our bodies are connecting, yet our minds are wandering in space.

My heart says I want you; your body shows that you feel the same way, too.

Though my mind doesn't care to leave a clue, I pray that this is a dream come true.

After a trip to ecstasy, I picture you laying next to me.

As I open my eyes, I realize that you're not there.

Hoping that my love does not turn to fatality, all I ask is that you turn my dream to a reality.

Love Is

Love is like a key to a door you may never find.

Love is like being born with 20/20 vision, but somehow, you end up blind.

Love is like a piece to a puzzle that will always be missing; it's like having a memory lost within your mind, but somehow, you end up reminiscing.

I feel so alone and like happiness is out of my reach.

I feel like I'm reading a book for a lesson that one can never teach.

Movie

Lights, camera, action, this scene is sure to bring pure satisfaction.

Perfect crew with the perfect cast, so why do I still feel stuck in the past?

Life is a movie that doesn't rewind; you just press play and let it all unwind.

You can't press pause if it's moving too fast—you just catch up and hope that the moment will last.

With time, every scene will mend.

Pressing stop will bring this movie to an end. Rewind isn't a feature that comes with time; you just press play and let it all unwind.

Our freshman year came and went quickly before my eyes. The closer it got to the end of the spring semester, the more I began pondering what my next move was going to be. Like a game of chess, every move is critical. I didn't have much to go back home to in Memphis and Anthony had one more year of high school left before he would graduate and come to Dallas for good. I had to prepare myself for my little brother's arrival, so I knew that I would definitely need to get an apartment and a car soon. Since school began, I had saved enough money to get an apartment and pay rent for the first few months. Between buying food and personal products, I had managed to save a good amount of money of money from my refund checks, but I would still need a job to keep up with my rental payments. The brainstorming had begun.

"Hey, Chrissy, do you know about any apartments around this area nearby the school?" I asked.

"Um, yeah. I know of Richardson Apartments and McCallum Highlands," she advised.

"Okay. Do you think you can take me to find an apartment?" I begged.

"Yeah, sure, girl! We can go now if you're done with class for the day," she cheerfully obliged.

"Yep, I sure am! Thank you so much!"

"You're welcome, hun. Let's check out Richardson first since they're closer," she recommended.

"Okay, cool," I agreed.

As we headed out of the dorm to the car, we ran into Nicole.

"Hey, where y'all going?" Nicole asked.

"Christine is taking me to find an apartment. You know the semester is almost over and I don't think that I'm going back to Memphis this summer. I'm just gonna find a job and work while I take one class during the summer semester. Do you want to go with us?" I offered.

"Nah, y'all go ahead. I have class in about an hour. I think that's pretty cool, though, that you gon' be getting an apartment," Nicole added.

"Yeah, Anthony will be finished with high school soon and he'll be coming to Dallas to live with me, so I need to get myself together. That's the promise I made him before I left for school," I explained.

"Aww, that's really sweet of you. You're a great big sister."

"Gee, thanks! Well, we will see ya later!"

"Okay, let me know how it goes."

"Alright, I will," I reassured.

The Richardson Apartments housing complex was fairly close to the school. The apartments were extremely nice, but a little on the pricey side of the fence.

As a college student, I needed to be on a strict, but also manageable, budget in order to survive.

"Chrissy, I like these apartments, but they're a little too expensive for me right now," I advised.

"Okay, I completely understand. Let's check out McCallum Highlands and see what they have to offer," she recommended.

"Alright, cool," I agreed.

McCallum Highlands didn't look like Richardson, but the price range was more up my alley. After getting an inside look at a one-bedroom apartment, I began filling out my application. A one-bedroom would have to do for me and Anthony, especially since I still had to get furniture for us to sit and sleep on. The clock was ticking and I knew that his senior year would go by much faster than I imagined. Just as we were walking out of the office, my phone rang.

"Hey, Ant!" I answered.

"What's up, sis? How's it going?" Anthony asked.

"Well, actually, I'm just now leaving an apartment complex. I went on a tour and put my application in!" I explained.

"Oh, word? That's what's up! I'm glad you gettin yo'self together like you promised. I can't wait to get out of this hell hole," he stated with hope in his voice.

"Yeah, I know. Don't worry, you'll make it through. Just one more year to go and it will be over!" I encouraged.

"Yeah, well, I damn sho' hope so! Mom's been trippin' and dis school shit ain't for me."

"I feel ya, lil bro, but you gotta hang in there."

"I'm trying, I swear I am. Mama put me out, so I been house hoppin'. Hopefully she'll get ova' herself and let me come back home," he continued.

"What? Why did she put you out?" I asked with concern.

"Man, you know how she is. Ain't shit changed with her since you left, Destiny."

"Well, what the hell has changed with you, Ant?"

"You know she don't keep too many groceries in the house and all she wanna do is get high, so I been gettin' it out here on my own," he explained.

"Anthony, please tell me you're not selling drugs."

"Man, sis, I gotta do what I gotta do by any means necessary. I don't have nobody to depend on! All I got is me!" he yelled.

Tears began flowing down my face as I listened to Anthony and watched his life flash before my eyes. He went from being my innocent, loving little brother to the average black male living in the ghetto.

"You will always have me, Ant. You know that! Please don't do this to yourself," I begged.

"As much as I don't want to, I have to, sis. Don't worry about me. I'll be a'ight. Keep ya head in them books, smart girl. I love you."

"I'm always gonna worry about you until you're down here with me. Please stay on the right track and don't drop out of school. Call me if you need me. I love you, bro."

"A'ight, I will." he agreed.

Before I knew it, I was sitting in Christine's car crying a river like there was no tomorrow. I couldn't believe that my brother was changing so drastically for the worst. He was my motivation to better myself and the reason behind me searching for an apartment for us to live in once he graduated, and now it seemed as though our goals were not going as planned. I had no one to turn to in hopes that they would help me and my brother. We were all we had as far as family goes.

Christine did her best to comfort me, but there was nothing she could possibly say to make me feel better about my situation.

After arriving back to the dorms, I wasn't in the mood to talk to anyone, so I locked myself in my room and cried myself to sleep.

Before I knew it, an hour had passed by the time I woke up. Donald had called my phone four times. I knew he had just what I needed: a shoulder to cry on and great advice. Without delay, I proceeded to call him back.

"Hey, beautiful," he answered.

"What's up? I was asleep when you called me earlier."

"Aww, okay. It's cool. I was tryna come see you, if that's alright with you," he asked.

"Yeah, dat's cool. Are you on ya way now?" I questioned.

"Yeah, I'll be there in about ten minutes," he confirmed.

"Okay, I'll be waiting in the lobby. That way, I can see when you pull up," I cheerfully stated.

"A'ight."

I eagerly jumped out of bed, freshened up before Donald arrived, and headed to the lobby shortly after. It wasn't long before I saw him pull up in his black F-150 truck with his music blasting. As I swiftly headed towards his truck, I saw that he had already been smoking kush in a Dutch cigar when he pulled up. As I opened the door, the smoke invaded the air.

"Hey, baby," I said as I greeted him with a warm, sensual kiss.

"'Sup, boo? You wanna hit dis?" he asked as he handed me the blunt.

"Hell, yeah. I need to," I responded as I reached for the cigar, inhaling as much as my lungs could possibly take in. I knew that I would begin to feel better about my conversation with Anthony today once I was high, or at least temporarily. We rode around and smoked two blunts back to back as we talked. I always enjoyed my time spent with Donald; he always knew just what to say.

"How was your day, baby?" he asked.

"It was a'ight, I guess. I went to class and Chrissy took me to fill out an application for an apartment."

"Oh, so you tryna move off campus?" he questioned.

"Yeah, my little brother will be graduating from high school next year and then he'll be moving down here, so I gotta get myself together before that time."

"Oh, that's what's up. I'm proud of you. You really doing ya thang out here. You know, if you need to crash at my place for a while, I don't mind," he offered.

"Gee, thanks, babe. I appreciate that. I'll let you know how it goes with the apartment, but I will definitely still need to get my own crib for my brother's sake," I explained.

"Yeah, I know. I'm just saying, if you needed to stay with me 'til that apartment came through for ya."

"Okay, cool. We'll see how that goes with the apartment first. So, how was your day?" I asked.

"Man, my day was straight. Same ol', same ol'. They worked the hell outta me today at work. My back hurting like a mothafucka."

"Aww, babe, I can give you a massage tonight once we get to your place," I offered.

"Oh, that sounds great! Are you hungry?"

"Nah, I'm good," I responded.

"Okay, well, I'mma stop at this gas station to get a couple more Dutches before we head to my crib. You want something outta here?"

"Yeah, just a bottle of water and some chips. Thanks."

"A'ight, cool," he answered as he exited the truck to enter the gas station.

By the time we arrived at Donald's apartment, I was as high as a kite. My eyes were so low that I could barely see out of them, and all of a sudden, I had the munchies. He assisted me to the couch and turned on the TV as he proceeded to roll up another blunt.

"Babe, there is something else that's been bothering me today that I didn't tell you in the car."

"What's that?" he asked.

"I spoke with my brother, Anthony, today, and I think he is selling drugs. I tried to talk him out of it, but he won't listen to me. I'm so afraid of losing him to street violence or to the jail. I'm trying not to let this stress me out, but I can't take my mind off of the possibilities of something going terribly wrong. I really hate the fact that he is just becoming another statistic in society instead of beating the odds and becoming successful."

"Don't let it get to you, baby. There comes a time in every man's life where he has to make a few decisions that force him to stand on his own two feet. Many people may not like those choices, but that's something that he will have to deal with, especially since his decisions come with consequences and repercussions," he encouraged.

"Yeah, but his decisions affect me, too. If something were to happen to him, I don't know what I would do without him," I explained with concern.

"But you can't let those thoughts get the best of you. Otherwise, you gon' end up in the crazy house and I can't be coming to visit you there," he joked, attempting to make me laugh.

"Oh, yes you would!" I smiled.

"For real, though, ya brother gon' be a'ight. Just keep letting him know that he has you to talk to and depend on, and that he needs to finish school so he can come down here to better himself," he explained as he lit the blunt.

"Okay, I will. I'll try not to stress about it so much. School needs my undivided attention right now, especially since finals are quickly arriving."

"Yep, dat's right. Keep ya head in dem books, bookworm," he laughed. "Whatever," I laughed.

"So, you gon' gimme my massage or what?" he asked as he exhaled the weed smoke out of his nostrils and stared into my eyes.

"Yep, come on. Let's go to your room," I suggested as I rose up off of the couch and proceeded to his room.

He put his blunt out and followed my lead while taking his shirt off. I gently guided him to lay on his stomach once we reached the bed. I sensually began massaging his shoulders and his back, relieving him of any stress that he was harboring. Once I finished massaging his back, he slowly turned around so that I was now on top of him. Before I knew it, we began kissing and grinding on each other, signaling that both of us were ready to be pleased. I slid my shirt off and tossed it onto the floor as he followed my lead. I began to softly tongue kiss him and slowly worked my way down his chest, leading to his already erect dick. I removed his pants and his Ralph Lauren briefs and began inserting his long, hard penis into my mouth, working it all the way deep into my throat and pleasuring him. Back and forth, I worked his erection in and out of my mouth before he reached the peak of his pleasure. He slowly slid himself out of my mouth, gently laid me on my back, and removed my bra and panties. He sucked and licked on both of my breasts before leading down to my thighs, kissing and licking them. Before I knew it, he was pleasuring me with his tongue against my clitoris, forcing me to erupt in ecstasy quickly. After reaching my climax, he climbed on top of me, slid his dick inside of me, and began slowly making love to me in the most passionate way that he ever had. I came over and over again as he thrusted in and out of me and kissed my neck. It wasn't long before he exploded inside of the condom. The night ended with three rounds of lovemaking and him holding me until we both fell asleep. Nights like these reminded me why I was so in love with Donald and why he was the best choice over any other man in my life.

CHAPTER 6

Where Were You

All of this seems so new to me.

I feel like an inmate being set free.

In a world full of people, I still feel so much misery, kinda like a captured dove begging to be set free.

Where were you when I felt all alone?

Where were you when I had no place to call home?

Where were you when I was isolated from family and friends?

Where were you when my heart was shattered and couldn't mend?

Where were you when I was living like a nomad?

Where were your donations when pennies were all that I had?

So, where were you when my world came tumbling down?

Take a look around and you'll see that you were nowhere to be found.

Misunderstood

Life is a blank verse; I wouldn't read it if I could.

I'm walking this rugged turf feeling so misunderstood.

It's like the sun with no shine; it's my heart on the line.

It's my life being written in just one line; I couldn't claim it even if it was mine.

It's being nice but knowing that these niggas is lying.

It's laughing to keep from crying.

I paint a picture that will fit the frame, but still, I'm misunderstood like a charade game.

I'm the piece to the puzzle that was always missing.

It's like you're deaf 'cuz you're never listening.

I lay the map for you to find your way; but you still need light in the middle of the day.

What more can I do when I feel so misunderstood?

If I wrote it down, you wouldn't read it if you could.

Looking in the mirror, I'd say I look damn good, but truthfully, on the inside, I feel so misunderstood.

A month had passed by and I hadn't heard from Anthony. I tried calling his phone, but I kept getting his voicemail until the number was eventually disconnected. No one had heard from him in a few weeks and I began to panic, not knowing what the end result might be.

Finals had arrived and I was losing focus rapidly. I finally got approved to move into my apartment by the end of the semester. Just when I thought that things couldn't get any worse, my phone rang. It was my mom. I hadn't talked to her the entire spring semester due to her drug addiction and absence in my college life.

"Hello," I cautiously answered.

"Destiny! Hey, baby girl. How you been?" she asked, sounding a bit slurred as if she were high.

"I'm alright, just studying for finals right now. How are you?"

"Oh, honey, I'm okay. Besides the everyday struggles I go through, I'll be a'ight. Are you coming home this summer? I know you didn't want to come home for Christmas break and spring break, but I would love to see my baby girl. I miss you so much," she begged.

A long awkward pause fell between us. I guess it was the shock of actually hearing my addict mother, who was currently high and trying to mask it, actually admitting that she missed me. Contemplating my answer, I slowly responded, all the while knowing that I was making moves in my life to progress without the help of any family and that I refused to let anyone hold me back. Most college kids had the love and support of their family while away at college, but that was an area that I lacked in. I knew I had to make my next move my best move because I had no one to depend on. I knew it would be a long time before I returned to Memphis for any reason.

"I'm glad to hear that my absence has been noticed, let alone missed. But no, ma, I won't be coming home this summer, or anytime soon for that matter. In fact, I'm moving into my apartment this summer and I have a few leads on some jobs. I'm working on getting myself together before I come back to visit," I proudly explained.

The despair from my mother's heart echoed through her voice as she came to realize that I may never return home. She began weeping as she tried her best to hide it when responding.

"Apartment? Don't you wanna come home? I've missed you since you've been gone. Why aren't you staying on campus anymore?" she sniffled.

"Because Anthony is moving down here when he graduates high school. I need to have everything ready for our new life when he does," I explained.

"But, but, what about me? I'm y'all's mother. How you just gon' leave me like dat?" she stuttered.

"You seem to be doing just fine without us so far, but you're welcome to come visit after you check yourself into a rehab center and complete the program. We love you, ma, but we're tired of your antics. Anthony hasn't had a place to live because you keep putting him out; that's why he's gon' move here to get himself together. He'll always have a home here with me. Speaking of my brother, where is he? I can't get a hold of him and no one seems to know where he is! Maybe if you stopped putting him out, we wouldn't have this problem!" I began yelling out of pure frustration.

"I am still your mother, little girl, and you ain't gon' talk to me like I'm a damn stranger! It ain't my damn fault Anthony wanna run the damn streets with all dem gangbangers and drug dealers! If you had bothered to ask me, you could have gotten my side of the story and not just his! Anthony has been selling drugs and robbing people. He was picked up by the police about a week ago.

He's still locked up 'cuz he ain't got no bail money right now. I'm doing the best I can to get him out, ya know!" she yelled.

Silence fell on the phone for a moment between us as tears began falling down my face. One of my worst fears had become a reality. My brother had become a statistic and was now part taking in criminal activity.

"What do you mean, he's locked up? Why hasn't anybody called me?" I sniffled.

"Ant called me a few days ago and told me what was going on. He said that he would call you soon. He doesn't want you to worry and stress. You have tests to study for," she urged.

"Yeah, well, he doesn't get to tell me what I need to worry about, especially when he's going down the wrong path," I angrily responded.

"Well, he's gon' do what he wanna do. All we can do is be there to pick up the pieces when he needs us. He won't listen to anyone but himself," she nonchalantly stated.

"With that kind of attitude, why should he listen to you? You're his mother and you sound like you've already given up on him. I'm always gonna believe that he can change and turn his life around. There is still a chance as long as he is still alive."

"I ain't givin' up hope. I'm just being logical about the current actions he has shown me," she responded.

"Yeah, well, what has your use of cocaine said about you as a mother? What has you not showing up to my graduation said about you? There are a lot of things that we could go back and forth about regarding our actions, but my point is that we're all human and everyone makes mistakes. Everyone deserves a chance, that's all I'm saying," I explained.

"I hear you, but some people never change, no matter how hard you try to help them," she hypocritically stated.

"Yeah, tell me about it," I sarcastically stated. Her words were a reflection of her own actions.

She never truly grasped the concept of what a parent should be; she always remained distant and self-absorbed as if her children were not affected by her actions.

"Well, I gotta go. I'll talk to ya some other time," she said, ending the conversation as she rushed off the phone.

"Okay, please let Anthony know that he needs to call me," I urged.

"Alright, I'll tell him. Bye, baby girl."

"Bye, mama," I replied as I ended the call, only to bury my face into my pillow and release a river of tears.

I couldn't fathom what my life would be like without Ant. It seemed as though everything I was doing to improve our lives was insufficient and in vain. How could he do such things? Did he not think about me and our plans to better our lives? What pushed him over the edge to turn to crime and gang activity as a way out? My mind was racing a million miles a minute with a ton of questions that only Ant could answer. Crying a river wouldn't fix the problem. Falling behind in my schoolwork sure as hell wasn't an option and would never benefit me. The only two things that I could do were fall to my knees and pray, and wait by the phone for Ant to call me.

To distract me from my problems, the only productive option I had was to bury myself into my schoolwork. Preparing for finals was the only priority that I had control of; school was my life and there was nothing that could prevent me from succeeding and graduating except for me. A week filled with final exams flew by faster than I dared to believe. I still had one more exam to take before it was complete, not to mention that I still hadn't heard from Ant or my mother.

On a beautiful, sunny day, as I left the dorm and began my walk to campus to take my last exam of freshman year, my phone rang unexpectedly.

"Hello," I answered.

"What up, sis?"

"Anthony?"

"Yeah, it's me. Who else could it be?" he joked, trying to lighten the mood.

"Where are you? Are you okay?" I anxiously quizzed him.

"I'm cool, I'm still locked up. I told moms to tell you," he explained with disappointment in his voice.

"Yeah, she did tell me, but I would rather hear it from you to get the truth about what's going on," I enlightened him while trying to remain calm.

"Man, you already know da deal with me. I had to do what it takes to survive in these streets."

"That's not the definition of a man, Ant. You don't have anything to prove to anyone. A man stands on his own two feet without needing validation from anyone else. I'm down here busting my ass to make sure that we have a better life than the one that we were given and yo' ass is out here gang banging and selling dope!" I explained with fury and frustration.

"Chill out, man. I'mma be good. I'm doing the best I can to make sure I make it down there wit'chu," he pleaded.

"Living the thug life is not doing the best you can! Going to school, graduating with your diploma, and staying on the right track is doing the best you can! Don't feed me that bullshit 'cuz I'm not buying it!" I yelled.

"Hold da hell up, Destiny! You don't know shit about what I been going through! You got yo' nose in da air like you better than somebody 'cuz you going to school! FUCK SCHOOL! School wasn't there for me when I was gettin' my ass beat at school. You damn sho' wasn't there for me when moms was puttin' me out on da streets! Nobody fed me, nobody showed me love until I found my Bloods, so from here on out it's bloodline til I die!" he yelled at the top of his lungs with rage.

Tears began falling down my face as I listened to my little brother throw his life away. He had now dedicated himself to a gang and a life of crime. I had no time to fall apart as I was slowly approaching my class, which would begin shortly.

"I don't understand what has happened to you. I feel like I don't know you. Please don't do this, Ant. I love you, but the road that you're on only has two exits: prison or death. You have control of your future, but it starts with the decisions you make today," I sniffled as I begged and pleaded.

"I hear you, sis. I love you, too, but it's my life. Ain't nobody been there for me all this time, so I'll be a'ight. I'm just tryna maintain 'til I get the hell outta here. I see the judge on Monday, so I should be gettin' outta here soon."

"I feel like you're pushing me further away from you and out of your life just because I'm in Texas tryna better myself. That's not fair to me; you know you will always have me in your corner. You don't hear me complaining about being down here all alone with no help in sight, but I deal with it because it's what I have to do. I hope and pray that you find your way. Until then, when you get out, please go back to school so that you graduate on time. You can't come down here to better yourself 'til you finish school. You need to make that your first priority."

"Okay, sis, I will. I'll try to keep you posted on what's going on, but don't worry and stress about me. I'mma be a'ight."

"Alright, well, I gotta go. I just got to class to take my last final exam. I love you."

"I love you too, sis. Stay up."

I pulled myself together as I entered my class ten minutes before my exam, which gave me extra time to review and temporarily allowed me to forget about my conversation with Ant. Moments later, Dr. Swanson had entered the classroom and began handing out the exams.

CHAPTER 7

Too Good To Be True

It's like being one number away from winning a billion dollar lottery.

It's like holding a safe in your hand without having the key. It's like being first place in a never-ending race. It's like waking up every morning to an unknown face.

It's like being married but still unable to commit.

It's like finding the perfect dress, but it just won't fit.

It's like searching for something right before your eyes.

It's like knowing the truth but believing the lies.

It's like dying but you know you're gonna live for sure.

It's like having an incurable disease and waking up with a cure.

It's like buying a brand new pair of dirty shoes.

It's like winning a game the entire time, yet somehow, you lose.

Somehow, I've managed to fall head over hills for you, but just before I reach the bottom, I realize that some things are just too good to be true...

Hell No

It's the second time we've had this argument.

With all of your mistakes, I should have taken the hint.

I can't convince myself that I need you; I guess love is too good to be true.

How lucky you were to have someone so true? Maybe I should be sorry for forgiving you. It's not that I find myself missing you;

I just feel sorry for the next girl you're gonna lie to.

God couldn't answer my prayers with you in the way.

Now that you're gone, all I see is a brighter day.

I was as true as true can get.

No more cursing the day we met; no more wondering why this relationship could never be.

I couldn't see myself loving someone who doesn't love me.

I forgive you for lying, cheating, and breaking my heart.

Too bad you're the reason why we're apart.

This road, we've been down it before, but now, there's a dead end to forgiveness forevermore.

I will not sell myself short, nor will I settle for less.

From now on, my strength will be at its best.

You kept your lying and cheating on the low, and you're still asking,

Will you take me back?

HELL NO!

Through

Despite how wrong you treated me, I never thought I would ever be through.

I chose to forgive you because I wanted to be with you.

You walked into a door that will never open again, but because of your careless actions, you just lost a true friend.

Maybe you don't know what it means to be loyal and true, but I do know that I will no longer be with you.

You put me through heartache and pain, and now, your problems will no longer be on my brain.

You went against what it meant to have a true relationship, but now I'm the one you won't be with.

I will no longer stress about my problems with you.

Still asking me, Why? Because I'm through!

Two months had passed into the summer and I was well on my way to having it all together. Donald and I were exclusive and I moved into my spacious one-bedroom apartment. In addition, Nicole's aunt had connections at the local children's clinic, so she was able to hook me up with a receptionist job. My job worked around my summer classes. I now had a steady paycheck, so I was able to buy a few things for my apartment. My life was finally coming together for the better, especially since Christine took me to get my driver's license. I discovered a new sense of security and independence. I began saving money for a car, but in the meantime, I relied on public transportation to get around, along with getting a ride from Donald or Christine every now and then. Anthony had finally been released from jail and had been attempting to go back to school to complete his senior year. Things were finally looking up for us.

After a long day at work, I called Donald to pick me up. He arrived just as I was walking out of the front entrance double doors.

"Hey, babe," I greeted him with a soft peck on the lips.

"What's up, boo? How was your day?" he asked.

"It was straight, nothing major. I'm exhausted and hungry,"

I giggled.

"You always hungry, fat girl. I swear there's a sumo wrestler

living inside of that skinny body of yours," he joked.

I laughed. "Yeah, well, she's trapped and I'm not lettin' her out! What have you been up to today?"

"Nothin' much. I was off work today, so I paid some bills and went to get an oil change on the truck. What'chu feel like eating?" he asked as he seductively glanced at me.

"Umm, I don't know," I hesitated as my stomach and my mind briefly deliberated. "Maybe pizza," I finally decided.

"A'ight. Pizza it is, baby," he cheerfully responded.

After stopping by the gas station to get drinks and swinging by the pizza place, we finally arrived at my place. After laying my purse on the counter and taking my five-inch stilettos off, I immediately headed straight to the shower, leaving Donald in the living room to get settled in. I finally joined him after a thirty-minute shower; as I entered the living room, I found him snoring on the couch with the pizza box laying wide open on the coffee table in front of him. I smiled, proceeded to fix my plate, and sat next to him without waking him.

Shortly after digging into my pepperoni pizza, Donald's phone lit up on the table, indicating that he had received a text message. Curiosity got the best of me. Who could be texting him this late at night? As I picked up his phone, I immediately zoomed in on the name that appeared on the screen: Jessica. She was definitely someone I knew nothing about. Luckily, he didn't have a password on his phone, so accessing the message was easy. The message simply read, "Hey baby." It wasn't much, but it told me everything that I needed to know about what kind of relationship they had going on. Not feeling the need to respond, I proceed to scroll through their conversations.

Before I knew it, I discovered what may decide the fate of our relationship. Jessica broke the news that she was pregnant with Donald's baby. His responses to her were seemingly joyful, making her feel all the more confident about having the baby in hopes of being one big, happy family.

A river of tears began streaming down my face. I couldn't believe what I was reading. How could my Mr. Wonderful turn out to be a false illusion? Was the baby even his? But if he doubted that it was, wouldn't he say so? So many thoughts and speculations ran through my mind. I didn't know what else to do besides cry. I knew that I couldn't approach the situation head-on because it was partially my fault that I found out. I had no right to snoop through his phone without his permission.

I felt intrusive but deceived at the same time. I knew that it would take some time for me to approach the situation correctly without being confrontational. I immediately exited out of his messages and placed his phone in the same exact spot that he had it in, then went to my bedroom to rest my brain and left him on the couch sound asleep.

The next day, I went about my day as if nothing happened. I couldn't fathom starting an argument with Donald knowing that I had no business reading his messages and snooping through his phone without his permission. Two wrongs don't make a right, but damn! Why the hell did it have to be me? Why did I have to find out this way? I knew that I had to face this situation head-on, but I just don't know how.

I finally gathered up the nerve to just do what was best for me, and that was to break up with Donald. I knew that it was his baby and I knew that he wanted to be with her; after all, the text messages said it all.

He denied it at first and tried to start an argument, but I dodged that entire situation by keeping it short and sweet and getting straight to the point. It hurt me more than ever to break up with him, but I knew that it was something that I needed to do for the sake of my sanity. I couldn't fathom having to deal with all the "baby mama drama" that would likely come. I had to move on with my life, even if it meant that I had to do it without him...

CHAPTER 8

Dead End

Sometimes, I have feelings and I don't know how to show them.

So, I wrote my feelings down for you in this poem.

I may not know where this story begins, but this heartbreak and forgiveness is where this nightmare ends.

Falling for you was never in my plans.

My tears have reached a dead end; I'm leaving it in God's hands.

You've hurt me in ways that you may never realize.

I thought you stole my heart, but you're just a thief... in disguise.

My heart is hurting from this pain that I feel.

This dead end is where my heart will begin to heal.

Speechless

It's like a mouth without a tongue.

I'm speechless without a breath in my lung.

I'm at a crossroad between my heart and reality, stuck between the outcome of what could or may never be.

All I ever wanted was for you to love me.

To confess my love for you is the only way I can be set free.

My heart is hurting and I can't let go.

Will my heart heal past this pain? Maybe I'll never know.

The way you made me feel was breathtaking; it can't be described.

What we shared was more than just a vibe.

When I'm with you, the world stops spinning.

Without you, I feel like I'm running a race that I'm not winning.

It's like speaking without a tongue; it's like hearing without your ears.

Sometimes, knowing the truth doesn't always help you face your fears.

It's like hugging without arms, running without legs, seeing without eyes.

It's like denying the truth, but believing the lies.

It's like writing a book without words; it's like flying in a sky without birds.

It's like a sun without light.

It reminds me of a war without the fight.

You held my heart, I must confess.

The way you made me feel, I'm speechless.

I'm not asking for a chance for us to give it another try—

I just needed closure for one last goodbye.

It was a beautiful Saturday evening. The sun was shining and the wind was blowing just right. A fellow classmate and I decided to go shopping while Nicole stayed back at my apartment. She wanted to use my place to see her new boo... whoever that was. She was already seeing Chris full-time, even though their relationship was a roller coaster—but then again, whose relationship isn't? But whoever this sideline guy was that she was now seeing, I had never met him before and she didn't talk much about him unless it had something to do with sex, so I figured it wouldn't last long. I was hopeful that she would get herself together enough to make things work with Chris, but as a loyal friend, I made it a point to never judge any of my friends and their situations. It wasn't like my relationship with Donald was peaches and cream, anyway, especially after I decided to stay with him after getting some other bitch pregnant and he still chose to leave my dumb ass.

Through it all, my girls Nicole andChristine stuck by my side and supported me without judgment, so it was only right that I did the same for them no matter what—even if that meant keeping their most horrific secrets and having their backs through it all. We had built an unbreakable sisterhood and bond that would stand the test of time without question... or so I thought.

As I got out of my classmate's car and she sped off into the sunset, I approached my apartment and turned the key to unlock the door. Just as I entered my apartment, I could smell the weed smoke thick in the air of my living room. Shoes had been left on the floor and my room door was closed. As I crept closer to the door, I could hear my bed squeaking. I slightly pushed the door open and I could see Nicole straddling Adrian!

My eyes couldn't believe what I was witnessing. Before I knew it, my mouth let out a horrific scream as I forcefully pushed the door open. My horrifying scream startled them so much that she stumbled off of him, nearly falling to the floor as she tried to cover her fully naked body in shame.

"WHAT DA HELL IS GOING ON HERE?!" I yelled full of rage and disgust. Not only was Nicole fucking our best friend's long-term boyfriend, but the bitch decided to do it in my damn bed.

How could she stoop so low to put our friendship with Christine at risk, especially after she had always been a loyal friend to the both of us?

"I am so sorry,Destiny," she explained while nervously attempting to get dressed.

"ADRIAN, WHAT DA FUCK ARE YOU DOING HERE FUCKING YOUR GIRLFRIEND'S BEST FRIEND?! YOU'RE THE SCUM OF THE EARTH!" I continued to scream at the top of my lungs in mere disgust and disappointment.

Trembling from nervousness and the complete shock of being caught , he stuttered while dressing himself, "I'm so, so sorry, Destiny. Please, please don't tell Chrissy," he pleaded.

"You don't damn worry about what the hell I tell Chrissy!

And if you're a smart man, you'd better tell her first before I DO!" I shouted furiously .

"I don't wanna break her heart. I love her," he cried.

"Well, if either of you cared about her at all, you two wouldn't be fucking—especially not in my bed,!" I said, pointing at the two of them to assure that neither of them was exempt from that statement.

"Just let me explain, Destiny," Nicole pleaded.

"What is there to explain, Nikki? I saw what I needed to see. Adrian, I think you need to go now!" I instructed as I pointed to the door.

He got dressed rather swiftly without speaking a single word and quickly exited my apartment without even saying goodbye to Nicole. After I locked the door behind Adrian, I waited in my living room for Nicole while she got dressed. She had some explaining to do for her careless actions. My head was spinning and I just didn't understand how someone who called herself a friend could do something so reckless, knowing how badly this would hurt Christine, especially if she ever found out...

"I am so sorry, Destiny. I never meant to hurt you," Nicole explained as she entered the living room, pulling her jeans up.

"I am the last person you should be concerned about hurting. You should have had Christine in mind instead," I scolded.

"I know. I feel like shit. I don't deserve friends as good as you guys," she said as she held her head down to the floor while sitting next to me on the couch.

"You should feel like shit! We would have never done anything like that to you," I explained.

"I don't know anything else other than to be this way. I can't help it!" she cried.

"What do you mean, Nikki?" I asked, confused and frustrated. How could she not take responsibility for her own actions and the role she played in this whole thing?

"All of my life, no one ever gave a damn about me. I was raped when I was twelve!" she screamed.

Speechless with my mouth wide open, I listened as she carried on to explain.

"My mother never paid much attention to me because she was either running the streets behind her latest boyfriend or she was working two jobs. It was a rainy, dark winter night when he crept in," she sniffled, then paused.

"Who crept in, Nikki?" I asked as I rubbed her back, attempting to comfort her.

"My Uncle James," she sobbed even harder, before continuing.

"He had touched me inappropriately before, but I was always too afraid to tell on him. I knew that my mom wouldn't believe me; she always called me a liar when I tried to tell her something, but this time, he took it too far. He crept into the bed with me while I was sleeping and began to caress my butt while slowly sliding my panties down. When I awoke, he was on top of me with an erection. He pressed his hand over my mouth so that I couldn't scream. He then forced himself inside of me as I tried my hardest to fight back with my weak arms and legs.

I was robbed of my innocence in a matter of seconds by someone who practically helped my mother raise me." She let out a whaling cry that will forever ring inside my ear from the pain that it carried.

I couldn't imagine what she must have been going through, carrying such a heavy burden around all by herself. No wonder her confidence and self-esteem were below the dirt. She couldn't trust anyone, not even her mother's brother—or her mother, for that matter. Her promiscuous ways were now explained and better understood—not excused, but understood. How could someone who is supposed to be a family member do such a horrible thing to an innocent child? My mind ran a million miles a minute as I consoled my friend in her time of need. I had no words that would begin to be good enough for my dear friend, so we sat in silence as we cried together for the next thirty minutes or so. Finally I turned to her and said, "I am so sorry that this happened to you, Nikki. I will always be here for you, no matter what. Your secret is safe with me. I promise," I reassured.

"Thanks, Destiny. I appreciate it. Your friendship means everything to me," she sniffled.

"We will get through this together, and your secret about Adrian is safe with me, too. I'm sure you know what the right thing to do is," I assuredly glanced at her.

Holding her head down in shame and pity, she mumbled, "Yeah I know that I need to tell Chrissy and cut Adrian off. I will... just give me some time to figure things out. I promise I will tell her."

"Good, and time is of the essence. Nothing good may come from you revealing that but the truth will always set you free; remember that," I encouraged.

The end of our sophomore year in college had finally arrived and finals were two weeks away. I finally had a sense of balance in my life. Nicole had finally begun the healing process from the pain that her family caused in her life. She still hadn't told Christine what happened between her and Adrian out of fear of losing her as a friend, and ultimately, she did not know how to handle the situation.

It was a normal girls' night at my place, something we tried to do at least once a week together that consisted of movies, popcorn, weed smoke in the air, and a little girl talk. We were watching The Color Purple and as it came to an end, we all sobbed in unison. Suddenly, Nicole turned to me and Christine with a look of despair on her face.

"I have something to tell y'all," she admitted.

"What is it?" I asked.

"Yeah, what's up, Nikki?" Christine added.

"I'm pregnant," she shamefully admitted with her eyes full of tears.

Christine glanced at me with a face full of confusion. I returned the look before we both rushed to console Nikki.

"Oh, no! Don't cry, Nikki! You'll be fine. You've got us if no one else cares. We've got your back, girl," Christine assured her.

"How far along are you? And are you gonna keep it?" I asked, trying to be as gentle as possible.

She looked up, lost and unaware of what she wanted out of life. "I don't know... How am I gonna finish college with a baby?" she questioned.

"Girl, anything is possible with God and the right people in ya corner," Christine explained.

Christine always knew just what to say; she was always the optimistic one in the group. Maybe it was because she was raised in a two-parent home and never wanted for anything, and so her outlook on life was jaded by a fairytale myth that the whole world was this way.

Her optimism always came in handy especially during our times of need.

"She's right, Nikki. Anything is possible—all you have to do is believe and have faith," I assured her.

"I just wanna die! My life couldn't get any worse than this, man!" she cried.

"Death is worse than this, Nikki. Don't talk like that. We need you, and that baby needs you," Christine explained.

"Who is the father, Nikki?" I asked out of curiosity. She gave me a look of uncertainty before answering.

"I don't know," she sobbed.

Christine and I glanced at each other in despair for our friend. We had no idea what she was going through. All we knew was that we had to be there for her the whole way through.

But then, I thought to myself silently, could the father be Adrian? I mean, she did have an affair with him and still hasn't told Christine. I wonder if Adrian knows yet. Maybe she won't tell him. Then again, maybe the baby wasn't his...

"Everything will be fine, Nikki," I said as I rubbed her back gently.

"Yeah, girl! There are a lot of girls who get pregnant before finishing college and they manage to make it through," Christine encouraged.

Nicole just looked at her with a blank look as if she had no clue what was to come in the near future. We sat in my living room for three hours comforting Nicole in her time of need. It wasn't long before we were laid out snoring on the couch and the floor after crying with her.

A month had passed and Nicole's stomach hadn't gotten much bigger since we first discovered her pregnancy. While watching TV at my place, just the two of us, I turned to her.

"How is the pregnancy going, Nikki?"

"I had an abortion," she admitted while holding her head down in shame.

"WHAT?!" I screamed.

"I had to! I didn't have a choice, and Adrian didn't want the baby, so he paid for me to have an abortion," she cried.

"Fuck him and his wants! So, you did know who the father was, you just didn't want to tell me!" I yelled out of frustration.

"It's not that I didn't want to tell you. I just didn't want to say it in front of Chrissy. She would have been devastated," she explained.

"That's a sorry excuse if you ask me, Nikki. The entire situation is completely fucked up already. Chrissy is going to be devastated in the end no matter what because she loses on both ends. No need in trying to spare her now. You might as well get it over with," I honestly stated.

"I know; you're right. I have to tell her. I will... I just need some time," she pleaded.

"You have had more than enough time to figure it out if you ask me. But whatever, you're gonna do what you want anyway. You caused all of this mess in the first place, so be a woman and deal with it! As your true friend, I have an obligation to keep it real with you and tell you the truth, even if it hurts," I explained.

"I know it's all my fault that I'm in this position in the first

place. I have to make things right no matter what. I appreciate you for being honest enough to tell me the truth, but loyal enough not to tell Chrissy before I get a chance to confess to her what I did," she admitted.

"That's what I'm here for," I assured her.

CHAPTER 9

Truth

Sitting in this chair, alone in this booth, just me, myself, and I alone facing the truth.

I love you, truth, because you keep it real.

I hate you, truth. You're the reason my heart will never heal.

They say time heals all wounds. Well, let time pass, and let it pass soon.

I love you more than I did yesterday;

I love you more than words can say.

This booth is crowded with silence and I feel so alone, so away from the world. I want to pack my bags and stay gone.

I loved you when no one else cared.

I split mine with you 50/50 when no one else shared.

I loved you for you and nothing less.

Even if you're not with me, I wish you the best.

Every day, I face the truth in my own way.

Every day, I realize that the truth didn't make you stay.

Keep Holding On

Sometimes in life, we face pain, joy, and sorrow, but keep your faith in God 'cuz there is always hope for tomorrow.

Even when you feel like there's nothing else that you can bare hold on to God's unchanging hand because He's always there.

When you're down on your knees and you feel like you can't make it through, lift your head to the sky and know that it is God's footprints that are carrying you.

So, even when you're weak and you don't feel strong, just keep the faith and keep holding on.

I'm Missing You

I miss you like the day without the sun, reminiscing on the days we shared that were the most fun.

I miss you like the night with no moon, staring out the window hoping you come back soon.

I miss you like an eye with no sight, praying that one day, you will finally see the light.

I need you like Eve needed Adam.

Being without you, I just can't fathom.

I need you like a heart needs a beat;

I need to know will our hearts ever meet.

I miss you like a poem with no words.

I need you like a voice that needs to be heard.

I'm missing you like I've never missed you before.

I need you to mend my broken heart that was once left torn.

Sophomore year came and went, and so did final exams. My summer had officially begun and was in full effect. I managed to end the semester with a 3.20 GPA and summer school was a no-go for me. I needed a break to free my mind from all the drama and frustration that took place during the school year. I had no intention of going back to Memphis to visit my Mom and I hadn't heard from Anthony since he was released from jail. I was sure that he kept his promise he made to me to finish school and stay out of trouble. After all, he was my baby brother and he wouldn't lie to me...

While getting a ride from Christine to work, my phone rang. The call was from an unrecognized number with a 901 area code—Memphis. As I answered the phone, I heard a woman screaming at the top of her lungs and crying.

"Hello" I answered.

"DESTINY, YOU GOTTA COME HOME NOW!" she screamed.

I recognized the voice instantly—it was my mother. The hurt and agonizing pain in her voice told me everything that I needed to know. I knew that it had something to do with Ant. Before she even finished her sentence, my heart fell into my stomach.

"What happened?" I asked.

"It's Anthony!" she yelled.

Unsure what would come out of her mouth next, I took a deep breath and braced myself out of fear.

"What about Ant, ma? Is he okay?" I frantically asked. "He's been shot and he didn't make it," she cried.

Silence fell over the phone and everything seemed to go inslow motion. Before I knew it, my phone hit the floor and I blacked out for a moment. My head was spinning and my heart was pounding a million miles per minute at the bottom of my stomach. The horrifying cry that I let out was powerful enough to be heard and felt a million miles away. I couldn't believe what I was hearing; I didn't want to believe what she was saying. I had to have been dreaming. This wasn't real. Not one bit of it was real. My hands were shaking so badly that I couldn't hold the phone. By now, Christine had pulled over on the side of the road and was attempting to comfort me. She was unaware of what was going on, but the look on my face said it all. Without asking any questions, she consoled me as I cried like a newborn baby in her arms for thirty minutes.

Finally, I was able to mumble a few jumbled sentences together and explain to Christine what my ears never wanted to hear.

"My little brother, Anthony, was shot and killed in Memphis," I mumbled.

"Oh, no! I'm so sorry, Destiny. I'm here for you for whatever you need," she cried.

I sniffled, "Thanks, Chrissy. I need all of the support I can get right now."

"Well, if you need a ride to Memphis, I can drive you, or my parents can buy you a plane ticket—whatever you need. You let me know what you wanna do and I've got you," she promised.

"Okay, just give me a few hours to figure out what I gotta do. I can't go to work like this, though. I'mma have to call in," I explained through my non-stop flowing of silent tears.

"I'm sure they will understand, and if they don't, fuck 'em," she assured me in an attempt to lighten the situation.

After taking a few moments to get myself together, I had to prepare myself to notify my boss. I picked up the phone to call my job to inform them of my brother's death; I let them know that I would need at least one week off in order to be there for my mother during this time. They assured me that my job would be secure until I returned and they offered me more time off if I needed it.

My head was still spinning in a whirlwind as Christine drove me back to my apartment to pack up and gather my thoughts. Having a friend like her seemed so surreal, yet so perfect; I wouldn't have it any other way. I was truly blessed by the best in the midst of all the turmoil in my life. I had loyal and true friends who would have my back no matter what situation I was in, and to me, that was worth more than anything.

As we approached my apartment, I swung open the passenger door to Chrissy's car in an attempt to get out, but I began vomiting on the curb before my feet could touch the pavement . Not only was my mind a wreck from the horrific news, but my body was also in a state of distress. My body couldn't process the news, nor could my mind or my heart. I was a wreck. How was I supposed to finish school when my whole reason for wanting to be successful was taken away from me? It's the unsaid goodbye that was killing me the most on the inside; it flowed from my heart through my tears. How was I supposed to get through this, a feeling that was so familiar, yet so foreign and new to me? I was used to being let down and feeling alone, but I always had Ant there for me. But now...

Christine helped me into my apartment and unlocked the door to help me onto the couch.

"Sit here. I'mma go get you some water," she instructed. "Okay, thanks," I gratefully stated.

She returned to the living room with an ice-cold bottle of water and sat beside me on the couch.

"You just let me know what you need and I'mma get it for you. You just rest your pretty little head, girl," she giggled in an attempt to cheer me up temporarily.

"I'm okay. I just need to rest and get my head together. I know that I have to pack up and head down to Memphis soon, at least by tomorrow. My mama needs me," I explained.

"I really wanna be there for you, Destiny. I don't mind driving my car—it's only six and a half hours away. I know you could use the support, and maybe Nikki can join us if she wants to be there for support, too. You know we will always have your back. That's what friends are for," she convincingly stated.

"That might be the route that would be best for me. It would give me time to prepare my mind for what I'm about to face," I agreed.

Luckily, I had paid my rent for the summer with my spring semester refund check and I had just gotten paid from work, so I had a little extra cash to spare for my traveling expenses of gas, hotel, and food costs. I knew that

I wasn't going to take my girls to the roach-infested shack my mother raised me and Anthony in; if she still had it, that is. I was almost too embarrassed to even show them where I was from because of the lack of stability that my mother had compared to Christine's parents. But I knew that they were my true friends, so I didn't have to worry about them being too judgmental over a situation that I had no control over.

"Okay, good. I'll get my things packed later today and we can leave first thing in the morning," she cheerfully stated as if she had a good reason to be excited. She was probably just happy that I agreed to let her drive me to my hometown, somewhere she had never been before. She insisted on helping me pack my clothes for the week that we would be gone. Against my will, she took out my suitcase and proceeded to my closet, taking out dresses and skirts that she thought would be suitable for the trip. At times like these, I can appreciate Christine's assertiveness; her spirits silently lifted mine. I quietly laid on the couch until I cried myself to sleep.

When I woke up, Nicole was sitting across from me on the love seat, staring at me and crying. What could she be crying about this time? I thought to myself. God knows that I didn't have anything left to give anyone else right now, especially not words of encouragement for whatever she was going through.

"Hey, Nikki, what's going on?" I asked.

She immediately rushed over to me and began consoling me and apologizing for what happened to Ant. Christine must have already filled her in on what was going on.

She sniffled. "Chrissy told me what happened."

Tears began to fall from my swollen eyes once again. "Thanks, Nikki. I need all of the support that I can get."

"I'm here for whatever you need, boo. When is the funeral?" she asked.

"Umm, I don't know anything just yet. All I know is that I have to get back to Memphis ASAP for my mama. She is all over the place like me right now," I sobbed.

"Okay, well, do you want me to go with you and Chrissy down there?" she asked.

"Sure, that will be fine, as long as it doesn't interfere with what you have going on 'cuz we'll be gone for about a week," I informed her.

"Don't worry, I'll be fine. I just want to be there for you like you've always been for me."

"Thanks, Nikki. I appreciate you," I gratefully stated.

Shortly after talking to Nicole, Christine walked through my apartment door with a suitcase and a small duffle bag.

Relieved that my sobbing had temporarily ceased, she immediately placed her bags by the coffee table and came to sit on the couch with us.

"OMG, you're awake and smiling!" she cheerfully stated.

"Yeah. Nikki said that she's gonna go with us to Memphis in the morning," I informed her.

"Oh, damn, we're leaving in the morning? I need to go pack my shit now!" Nicole jokingly stated.

We laughed at her efforts to lighten the seriousness of the conversation.

"Yeah, girl. We're gonna spend the night here at Destiny's place, then we'll leave at around 6:30 in the morning," Christine instructed.

"Okay, that's cool. I just need to go pack a few things. Will you give me a ride, Chrissy?" Nicole asked.

"Yeah, girl, that's fine. Destiny, you can ride with us. Then, we'll pick up something to eat on the way back," Christine explained.

"Nah, I'm good. Y'all go ahead," I urged.

"Hell nah! Get yo' ass up off that couch and come on with us! You don't need to be sitting in this apartment by yourself! At least come just for the ride, maybe that will ease ya mind. Nah, I know what's gon' ease ya mind!" Nicole laughed.

"Okay, I'll ride," I reluctantly agreed.

"Chrissy, we need to stop by Antoine's crib to get some loud on the way back. We all need to smoke a blunt right about now!" Nicole instructed.

"I feel ya! Y'all know I don't normally smoke with y'all, but I'mma hit the blunt tonight!" Christine explained.

We left my apartment immediately as the sun began to set. It wasn't long before Nicole had her things packed up and ready to go. We stopped by McDonald's to grab a bite to eat before heading to Antoine's house to pick up the weed. Just before arriving at my apartment, Nicole insisted that we stop at a nearby gas station to pick up a few cigars and snacks for when we get the munchies.

The rest of the night consisted of weed smoke in the air, laughs, and girl talk. Nights like these made me appreciate having good girlfriends who I could be myself around without the fear of being judged. They are the kind of friends who would always have my back no matter what phase of life that I might be going through; friends like that are hard to find. When I was a child, my mama always told me, "You ain't got no friends in life—remember that! But if you find one true friend in life, you're doing damn good!" I never understood that saying until now. During my childhood, I always struggled to fit in with the other kids in school, but I was bullied and I never had a boyfriend. It wasn't until I got to college that I really blossomed into who I really was, the girl who I'd always been afraid to show others for fear of rejection. I no longer had that fear as I realized who my true friends were, knowing that they would accept me no matter what. As I listened to Chrissy and Nikki, I couldn't help but think about Anthony. I missed him and I wasn't sure how I was gonna handle having to bury my baby brother.

All I knew was that God would give me the strength I needed to endure this situation. At this point, I was just grateful that I had sincere people who had my back through it all.

The next day, we left before the sun had completely risen. We loaded Christine's car with our luggage and snacks for the road as we prepared for the long six and a half-hour drive ahead of us. Christine drove for the first three hours before turning the wheel over to me. She trusted me driving her Benz, especially since she played a key role in me obtaining my license in the first place. I drove the rest of the way, which only made sense mainly because we were getting closer to Memphis. The closer we got to my hometown, the more I felt my heart sinking into my stomach and a lump growing in my throat.

We arrived in Memphis by 2 p.m. and nothing felt the same. The air smelled different, the sun shined differently upon the city, the grass didn't seem as green, and the birds didn't chirp the way I remember. I hadn't been back home since the day I left Anthony on the curb and rode off in a cab to begin my new life. Nothing in this city will ever be the same for me with Ant gone.

Soon afterwards, we checked into a suite at the Hilton on Ridge Lake Boulevard to accommodate the three of us with more than enough space during our stay. I couldn't fathom taking them to stay with my mom in that run-down apartment, especially after our lavish visit to Christine's home. When Christine's parents found out about Ant's death, they offered to pay half of our traveling costs and covered more than half of our hotel bill, which left us to split the small remaining amount between the three of us. After checking in, we all showered and changed our clothes before grabbing a bite to eat.

Shortly after eating, we went by my mom's apartment to see how things with the funeral arrangements were going. When we pulled up, there were multiple cars outside that looked familiar, much of which looked like a few of our distant relatives'. We didn't see each other often and they always talked about my mother behind her back because of her drug addiction. No one in our family was ever willing to help my mom with getting help for her drug addiction, nor did anyone step in to assist in helping take care of me and Anthony when we needed shelter or food. I felt like Anthony was all that I had in this world, and now that he was gone, I didn't see a point in even dealing with these so-called relatives of mine anymore. What's the point of having family if they aren't there for you when you need them, right?

But I guess them showing up to my mom's place was their way of being there.

"Well, this is it," I solemnly stated in an attempt to prepare the ladies for what they were about to see.

"Is this where you grew up?" Christine innocently asked.

"Yep, this is where I was raised: in the heart of the hood. I know it's not what you're used to seeing or being around, but this is the hand that life dealt me and I've tried to make the best of it," I explained.

"You don't have to explain anything to me, Destiny. I understand that no one has control of the environment that they are born in, nor the cards that life has dealt. That's what God is for, so He can change all that," she sincerely encouraged.

"Girl, your neighborhood looks better than mine!" Nicole jokingly stated in an attempt to lighten the mood. We laughed in unison as we got out of the car to head into my mom's apartment.

The scent of my mother's house crept through the doors before my Aunt Jackie even opened it. It reeked of fried catfish, liquor, and weed.

"HEY, NIECE! HOW YA BEEN, BABY GIRL?" she shouted as she greeted me with a hug and breath that smelled like two gallons of Hennessy.

"I'm alright, Auntie Jackie. These are my friends, Nicole and Christine," I stated as I swiftly introduced them.

I refused to let Auntie Jackie be the reason that I got embarrassed before being at my mom's house for a full five minutes, so they quickly spoke as I pulled them into the house in an attempt to avoid direct contact. I began looking for my mom before fully acknowledging anyone else who took up wasted space. I spotted her in the corner with a blunt in her mouth and a red plastic cup in the other. She was laughing with my Uncle Josh and my cousin Arnetta when she spotted me from across the room. A look of astonishment came over her face. She excused herself and quickly came to me, giving me the tightest hug I had ever received from her in my entire life. It's as if she was holding to the last piece of happiness that she had.

"Hey, baby girl! I've missed you. I'm so happy to see you!" she excitedly stated.

"Hey, Ma. These are my friends, Nicole and Christine."

She greeted them with hugs.

"How you been holding up, Ma?" I curiously asked as I searched her half-drunken eyes for answers to my question.

"I'm—I'm—I'm doing alright, baby," she stuttered.

"You know I'm here for whatever you need, Ma. I just want you to take care of yourself and seek help for the problems that you face outside of all of this mess," I urged.

"I know. I'mma get myself together once all of this funeral stuff is over with. I can't afford to lose my last child on this earth to anymore bullshit," she reluctantly admitted while glancing around the apartment searching for a way out of the conversation.

"Well, when is the funeral gonna be, Mama?"

"We are trying to see if Pastor Jones will let us get the church on Friday. That way, all of the other costs will be cheaper," she explained.

"Okay, good. How are you paying for all of this?" I asked.

"The church is raising money for us to pay for everything. So far, people have donated about $4,000.00"

"Okay, that's good. Well, I'mma head back to the hotel before it gets late. Tell everybody that I said 'hey,'" I stated as I gave her one last hug before leaving. I didn't acknowledge anyone else in the apartment.

"Okay, baby. Thanks for coming by. I'll see you soon, right?" she asked.

"Yeah. We'll come by tomorrow when everyone is gone," I reassured her.

"A'ight. It was nice meeting you girls," she said to Christine and Nicole as she gave them a goodbye hug.

"Nice meeting you, too. Sorry for your loss," Christine sincerely stated.

"Yeah, nice meeting you. I'm sorry for your loss too," followed Nicole.

We exited the apartment without anyone ever noticing that we were gone. Apparently, they were too drunk and high to notice anything—as usual.

Before we made it outside, tears began falling freely and uncontrollably from my eyes. I was hurt by the thought that my baby brother was no longer here, and that my mother was drowning her sorrows in drugs and alcohol as usual. She masked her hurt and pain by distracting herself with the laughter of everyone surrounding her. These were people who she knew wouldn't be there for long, but they temporarily were for the time being due to the occasion. Christine and Nicole silently understood the reason for my tears as we quietly rode back to the hotel.

The next few days were the hardest days of my life. Throughout the planning of the funeral, I was forced to recall every memory of Anthony, which made me miss him even more. On some days, Christine and Nicole bribed me that they would make me smoke a blunt if I didn't eat due to my lack of an appetite. Without them, I don't know how I would have made it this far.

The day of the funeral had swiftly arrived before I could even fathom the thought of the entire process. The day was gloomy and filled with so much pain. I struggled to dress myself for the funeral and food was not an option. The church managed to raise enough money to have a small funeral for Ant.

As we arrived outside of the church, I felt a sense of numbness as tears were continuously falling from my eyes. Christine and Nicole stood on each side of me and helped me into the church. The sanctuary was filled with sobbing relatives who didn't even show up to the house to offer moral support during this process. Not that they didn't deserve to grieve Ant, but how can you truly grieve someone that you never genuinely knew? Some of their faces were unrecognizable as we slowly walked past them. I found my mother bent over on the front row of the church hysterically losing her mind as my Aunt Jackie and Uncle Josh comforted her. We all quietly sat next to them as the service was about to begin.

The funeral processions were over quicker than I was prepared for.

I was glad when it was time to go to the cemetery, which meant that this nightmare was one step closer to being over. This pain was unbearable and I wasn't sure how much longer my body could withstand the stress and fatigue that this situation brought on.

We left the cemetery shortly after they began to throw the dirt on Ant's casket. I hugged my mother and said my last goodbyes to my baby brother. My heart was officially broken and faced the possibility of never being mended again...

We left Memphis the following morning. I couldn't fathom being there another day. The ride back to Texas was silently filled with relief that I had made it through this process with the help of my best friends. We talked about everything under the sun that could distract me from Anthony's death.

After arriving at my apartment, we immediately lit the last blunt that was left. Everyone was desperate for some kind of relief after that long, stressful trip, even Christine.

After a long week in Memphis, out of respect for my feelings, Christine and Nicole never mentioned Ant again unless I mentioned him or until I was willing to talk about him...

CHAPTER 10

Questions

So many questions racing through my mind.

You could read a thousand books, but the answers you won't find.

Trapped in between a fantasy and reality, not really knowing if this was how it's supposed to be.

Searching for the answers that I just can't find;

I stopped searching my heart and soul and began searching my mind.

God, please don't punish me. I'm only second guessing.

I'm navigating throughout life with so many questions.

I just hope that my decisions don't come with a permanent lesson.

Goodbye Part I

This is the hardest thing that I have ever had to do.

I'm not doing this just for me, but for you, too.

I really hate to have to say goodbye, but my heart won't let me stay and watch you cry.

There will never be another you, but if saying goodbye is the best thing, then I guess that's what

I will have to do.

There is no doubt in my mind how hard this may be, but I do know that this is killing me.

Looking back, I know what we had was real, but saying goodbye is the only way, with time, that my heart will heal.

Goodbye, goodbye, goodbye, farewell, goodbye. God knows I don't want to leave, especially while watching you cry.

You mean the world to me, but know matter how badly I want to stay, I know that I have to leave.

Standing in the mirror watching this person cry, while at the same time rehearsing how I must say goodbye…

Goodbye Part II

You said that it was true, I said it was lies.

You said hello, I said goodbye.

You played the games that I wrote.

No more taking you back and writing secret love notes.

I separate the gadgets from the toys;

I separate the men from the boys.

Never give more than you're willing to lose.

Now, it's my turn to pick and choose.

No more kisses goodnight; no more fighting for a relationship that's not worth the fight.

If broken hearts are hard to mend, then why are we standing face-to-face at this dead end?

Listening to every word you say, Reflecting back on that sad dark day, Asking myself, Why didn't I stay strong?

Who would have known that in love, there is no wrong?

Thinking back on the truth, the hurt, the tears, and the lies,

Saying to myself, This is the last goodbye...

Two months had passed since Anthony's death. Life wasn't easier, but I was going on with my life for his sake. After all, what did I really have to complain about? I was closer to graduating with my bachelor's degree, I had my own place, and I had a steady job that I truly enjoyed. Things were really looking up for me...

It was a typical Saturday at my place—loud burning in the air, my girls and I sitting around having our typical girl talk. Christine confided in us about how Adrian had been acting funny lately. As a result of Adrian's name being brought up in the conversation, Nicole had an uncomfortable facial expression.

"I mean, I don't know exactly what's going on with him. He hasn't touched me sexually lately and our phone conversations are beginning to get shorter and shorter," she confided in us.

"Well, have you tried asking him what's going on or what's different?" I asked.

"Yeah, but he just says that it's nothing and changes the subject. It's like he's uncomfortable talking to me," she explained.

Nicole sat silently listening without input, and then, it happened...

"I have something to tell you, Chrissy, but please don't be mad at me," Nicole mumbled shamefully.

"I can't guarantee you that at this point, Nikki, but I'll do my best. What is it?" Christine suspiciously stated.

"I slept with Adrian," Nicole confessed.

"YOU BITCH!" Christine screamed. She stood up and slapped

Nicole across the face so hard that her handprint appeared to be painted onto Nicole's skin.

I swiftly jumped in between the two of them to prevent a fight.

"I'm so sorry. It won't happen again. I didn't mean to hurt you,"

Nicole cried as she held the side of her face while lying on the floor.

"FUCK THAT! HOW COULD YOU DO THIS TO ME? IF YOU DIDN'T MEAN TO HURT ME, IT WOULD HAVE NEVER HAPPENED

IN THE FIRST PLACE, YOU CONNIVING LITTLE BITCH!" Christine hysterically yelled.

"Hold on, Chrissy. Just hear the girl out," I begged.

"So, you're on her side now?" Christine asked.

"No. I'm not saying that I agree with what she did; all I'm saying is, at least hear her out enough to decide what your next move will be. We have been through too much as friends to let some guy come in between any of us," I pleaded.

"Well, maybe you shoulda told that hoe that before she fucked my man!" she furiously explained.

"You're right in every aspect of how you feel. I just feel like we've been friends for too long to just let something like this ruin everything," I explained.

"She shoulda thought about that before she decided to try to take my place! You will never be me, you low-down, dirty, broke bitch!" she cried as she swiftly grabbed her things and headed closer to the door.

"Please don't leave, Chrissy," I begged with tears in my eyes.

"I don't really give a damn about what she has to say, Destiny, so save it," she stated as she slammed the front door and sped off in her car.

I silently turned to look at Nicole with dismay written all over my face. Why did she pick this time to confess to Christine? And was she truly sorry for what she did? Did she really stop sleeping with Adrian? What made her sleep with him in the first place, knowing that she was risking losing her friendship with Christine? My head was spinning; my heart was broken for the both of them. Although knowing Nicole's past didn't excuse her promiscuous and careless actions, it did help me to understand her a little bit better and have empathy for her situation. So many questions still hadn't been answered, but now was the time for her to tell the whole truth...

"What was that?" I asked.

"I don't know, Destiny, but I had to tell her. Too much time has already gone by. I just felt like it was the right time," she admitted.

"So, you chose to pull this stunt without telling me first?" I questioned.

"It wasn't a stunt. I just had to get it off my chest. It was killing me inside," she sniffled.

"Well, yo' ass shoulda thought about that before you fucked Adrian," I angrily explained.

"I know, but he made the first move on me! I know that's no excuse, though," she cried.

"I don't care if he made several moves on you. As Christine's friend, you shouldn't have reacted to him, and you should have let her handle him in the long run. It's called being a true friend, Nikki!"

"I know. I don't deserve friends like y'all," she sobbed.

"Well, you've gotta do something to get Chrissy to hear you out and get her to forgive you, if she decides to even befriend you again," I explained.

She glanced up at me. "Will you help me?" she asked.

"I can try, but I don't know how far we will get," I hopelessly explained.

Two weeks had passed and there was still no word from Christine. Nicole and I both called and texted her numerous times, but she refused to answer either one of us. I refused to give up...

While walking to my first class of the day on a beautiful Wednesday morning, I noticed Christine getting her books out of her car. I quickly walked over to her.

"Hey, boo!" I excitedly greeted her.

"Hey," she dryly responded with a look of surprise to see me. "How you been?" I asked.

"I'm good. Life goes on, ya know," she explained.

"Yeah, I know the feeling all too well. Listen, I'm sorry about what happened a few weeks ago, but you can't go on with life holding grudges and never facing the real issue at hand," I pleaded.

"It's a free country, Destiny; I can do whatever the hell I want. Don't lecture me about what's best for me, okay?" she sarcastically responded.

"I know, but I was hoping we could at least talk about it when you have the time," I begged.

"I'll think about it," she said. She glanced at me from the corner of her eye before walking away.

I never expected Christine to be so coldhearted, especially towards me of all people. I mean, what the hell did I do? I didn't sleep with Adrian, and I sure as hell didn't have

anything to do with Nicole sleeping with him or her telling Chrissy about it. I've always tried to do the right thing by both of them without getting in between this mess. I guess that doesn't matter when I probably look just as guilty as Nicole does. I just wanted to mend things between the three of us.

Three days later, Christine texted me agreeing to meet me at my apartment, but without Nicole being there. I agreed in the hopes that she would at least hear me out.

Before I knew it, I heard a knock at the door. I immediately knew that it was Christine. I hurriedly opened the door and greeted her with a smile and a warm hug.

"Hey, Chrissy!" I excitedly welcomed her inside.

"Hey, Destiny. How are you?" she asked as she returned the hug with a slight smile.

"I'm good, girl. How you been?" I asked.

"I've been taking things one day at a time since Adrian and I broke up," she immediately admitted.

"Yeah, I kinda saw that coming... he doesn't deserve someone as wonderful as you, anyway," I encouraged in an attempt to lift her spirits about the bad breakup.

"Yeah, I know, but it just hurts when someone you love hurts you so badly, you know?" She began to shed one tear after another at the thought of her heart being broken by Adrian.

"Yeah, I know, girl, but there are too many good men out there who are willing to give you what you want and need for you to be sitting around crying over that loser."

"I know, but I believed that he was the one," she cried.

"I know it hurts, but time heals all wounds. Just give it some time," I encouraged.

"Life just seems to have kicked me on every end with this situation. First, I lose my boyfriend, and as a result, I lose one of my best friends, too," she cried.

"Yeah, but you don't have to lose on that end, though. Nicole is so sorry for what she did. She has reached out to you to try to mend things."

"I know. I got her phone calls and text messages, but I just don't see how I can continue a friendship with her after she slept with my boyfriend. How am I supposed to trust her again?" she confided in me.

"I understand, and I don't blame you for feeling that way. With God's help, you can overcome this bump in the road. We all need each other to lean on when we feel weak and alone," I encouraged.

"I just need some time to get to a place where I can even look at her again, let alone talk through things without slapping her again," she said, slightly giggling at the silly thought.

"Yeah, we don't need no drama! Especially not up in my crib!" I laughed in an attempt to lighten the mood.

"I'm sorry about that. I didn't mean to put you in jeopardy of losing your place by nearly causing a fight," she apologetically confessed.

"Girl, you're good in my book. The cops weren't called and I wasn't evicted," I laughed.

"Can I ask you something?" she asked.

"Yeah, what's up?" I agreed.

"Did you know about Adrian and Nicole sleeping with each other?" she asked.

This was the question that I feared the most, because no matter what my reason for not telling her about them was, it wouldn't be enough to justify me not being a true friend to her on my end. I knew that I would look just as guilty as Nicole...

"Yeah, but I didn't know for the entire time that she was sleeping with him. It took me catching them in my bed for me to find out. It wasn't like she just came out and told me," I shamefully confessed.

"So, why didn't you tell me?" she curiously asked.

"When I found them in my bed, I cursed the both of them out and I put Adrian out. I told Nicole that she needed to tell you and that I would give her a sufficient amount of time to tell you, or else I would if she didn't," I explained.

"So, the both of them went months without telling me shit. That's messed up," she pondered out loud.

"Yeah, it is, but I don't want you to think that I was in on what they had going on. I would never do that to you," I pleaded.

"I would hope that you wouldn't; that's why I'm here. I believe that you've been a true friend to me. I can't just give up on our friendship and all that we've been through over this mess, especially when you were not involved," she admitted.

"Thanks for giving me the benefit of the doubt. I have always been a true friend to you. It gets tricky for me when situations like this happen, 'cuz I feel like I'm stuck in between you two and as if I have to choose between my best friends."

"You don't have to choose. I wouldn't put that kind of pressure on you to do that. All I ask is that you don't pressure me to speak to or be around Nicole until I'm ready," she requested.

"I understand. I can do that," I replied. "Thanks for understanding."

"No problem," I concurred.

We sat and talked for hours, just catching up on what had been happening in both of our lives over the course of the two weeks that we didn't see each other. She told me how she wasn't ever gonna see Adrian again because of his betrayal. It was a wonder to me how she had enough love in her heart to even fathom the thought of befriending Nicole again. But who was I to complain or question her feelings? After all, that was what I wanted. I was rooting for our friendship to make it through this obstacle. While simply listening to her and hearing her voice again, I realized that I really missed my friend and that I was so grateful to even call someone like her my friend. True friends are hard to come by.

CHAPTER 11

Make Believe

This love that I want seems like make-believe.

This void I feel is only making me leave.

I dream of the future every night, but somehow, this love just doesn't seem right.

This fairytale feels like a dream.

Sometimes in life, things aren't always what they seem

This love is flashing before my eyes; life's heartbreak is taking me by surprise.

These tears are shed from so many lies.

My heart is tired of so many goodbyes.

Where do I go from here, when reality doesn't seem so near?

Pain is what made me leave, and now, love, to me, is just make-believe.

Lesson Learned

Learn to live through the pain; learn to swim inside the rain; learn to walk the rugged turf; learn to ride the wave and surf.

This life I live has lessons learned.

Like going to school with no credits earned, what would I take from it if there was nothing to gain?

How can I learn when I feel like I'm going insane?

I feel like giving up. I can't take the pain and it's too much to stand the rain. I just don't see how I can walk the rugged turf but can't figure out how to surf. I went to school but learned nothing at all. Because there were no credits earned, I began to fall.

It's not worth it if there is nothing to gain. What good is an umbrella without the rain? What good is my mind if I'm going insane?

What can I learn from this dirty game?

Stay true to myself and never sell out for fame.

Playing with fire, you're going to get burned.

Learn to take the heat 'cuz life is a lesson learned.

Three months had gone by since Christine and I made up and she still wasn't ready to face Nicole. Their feud made it hard for me to spend time with them like I wanted to, so I had to split my time between the two of them equally. I enjoyed the personal bond that I have with each of them, but I just wished that things could go back to how they used to be. I wished we could all sit around and confide in one another, party, smoke, and just kick it like the good old days. Yeah, I miss those days. True friends are hard to come by in life and it hurts like hell every single day to be torn between the two.

I wished Nicole had never slept with Adrian and I wished that Christine wasn't so damn stubborn. But who knows? Maybe if he hadn't slept with Nikki, he would have just slept with some random chick and Chrissy never would have found out how much of an ass he really was. Everything happens for a reason, ya know...

It was a typical Tuesday and Chrissy and I were chillin' at my crib. We had just gotten in from a biology class that we had together, so we decided to go back to my place to study for an upcoming test. After only being there for thirty minutes, I heard a knock at my door. I wasn't expecting company and my phone hadn't rang.

"Who you got coming over? I thought we were supposed to be studying." Christine asked suspiciously.

"Da hell if I know. I didn't invite nobody over," I shrugged as I headed to the door.

As I peeped through the peephole, I could see Nicole standing there holding her head down.

"Oh, shit! it's Nikki!" I warned Chrissy.

"What da hell is she doing here? Did you set this up?" Christine furiously asked.

"Hell nah, I ain't set this up! I don't know what she's doing here!" I proclaimed.

"Well, I don't wanna see her trifling ass, so I'm leaving. I'll just catch up with you later," Chrissy said as she began to gather her books from the kitchen table.

"Just hold up a minute, Chrissy. You ain't gotta act like that. At least lemme see what she wants," I said as I opened the door.

Nicole stood there like a child in distress with tears in her eyes.

"Hey, Nikki. What's going on?" I asked in an attempt to find out what was going on.

"Hey, Destiny. I'm sorry for poppin' up without callin', but I really need to talk to you."

"Umm, okay, but Chrissy is already here and I'm not quite sure that now is the best time to talk," I explained in an attempt to deter her from staying.

"I understand, but I have something important that I need to tell you and I don't have anyone else who I can turn to," she cried.

"Okay, come on in," I hesitantly stated.

"Hey, Chrissy," Nicole sniffled.

Christine ignored her as she swiftly continued to pack up her belongings.

"What is it, Nikki? What's going on?" I anxiously asked.

She glanced up at Christine as she got closer to the door. "Chrissy, will you please stay? I need you right now more than I have ever needed anyone in my life. Just hear me out, and if you still feel the same way when I'm done, then I promise won't bother you anymore," Nicole begged with tears rapidly flowing from her eyes.

"What do you need me for? You have Destiny," Christine defiantly insisted on leaving.

"Things aren't the same without you! I know I fucked up. I never should have fucked Adrian! He wasn't worth losing you as a result of my mistakes. I am sorry from the bottom of my soul. I hope that you will receive that with love because I truly mean it. I never meant to hurt you. I don't know how to be as good of a friend to you as you and Destiny have been to me because I never really had true friends that felt more like sisters. I'm closer to y'all than I am to my own sisters. Y'all seem to understand me better than my own siblings do. I know that what I did was heartbreaking, selfish, and undeniably foolish. I promise you that if you give me another chance at friendship, I will show you how remorseful I really am and that I can be a good friend to you," Nicole poured her heart out with tears in her eyes.

For a moment, Chrissy stood still with a blank stare on her face in disbelief before speaking. "I hear what you're saying, Nikki, but only time will tell. I am still hurting from the whole thing because I am the only one in the situation who lost out on both ends of the equation."

"I know, but it doesn't have to be that way from this day forward. Just stay to hear me out because my life has taken a turn that I never thought it actually would," she pleaded.

"What do you mean, Nikki?" I interjected.

"What I mean is that I went to the doctor a few days ago and they told me that I was HIV-positive," she began sobbing even harder than before.

I couldn't believe what my ears had just heard. Christine dropped her bags and ran over to the couch to console Nikki with me. Was I dreaming? I hoped this was just a nightmare that I would soon wake up from and everything would go back to normal. I mean, I'd rather deal with the boyfriend drama that we were facing than to deal with one of my best friends having HIV. What was I supposed to say? What could I do? All I knew is that we had to be there for Nicole throughout this whole thing, no matter what. Somehow, this unbearable news made everything else that we were dealing with seem so small. As if nothing else mattered, Nicole's life being at risk now kind of put everything into perspective. The news certainly must have impacted Chrissy drastically, 'cuz she was crying and consoling Nikki as if nothing ever happened between her and Adrian. I was glad that we were able to come together, but it hurt that it took something so devastating to bring us together and make us put our differences to the side. We sat on the couch crying and hugging each other for an hour before any of us said a word.

"I'm so sorry that this happened to you, Nikki. I wish that there was something that I could do," I admitted.

"It's not your fault, Destiny. I should have been more mindful of who I was having sex with instead of being a slut," Nicole confessed.

"We will get through this together. We've got ya back for life," Christine encouraged.

"That means the world to me, Chrissy. I need y'all support right now more than ever," she gratefully explained.

"Well, you can count us in. We're in this together," Chrissy continued.

"Do you know who gave it to you?" I curiously asked.

"Honestly, I don't know if it was Chris or Adrian. I know that I slept with a lot of guys, but those were the main two that I went back and forth with recently since I last got checked," Nicole explained.

And there it was again. It seemed as if a dark cloud had entered the room as she uttered Adrian's name in the same sentence. Christine's face said it all: fear, anger, hurt, and confusion; the fear of not knowing if there was a possibility that she, too, could be infected with the HIV virus because of Adrian. Fear of the unknown was now beginning to sink in...

"So, you slept with Adrian raw?" Chrissy asked.

"Yeah," Nicole shamefully answered as she held her head down.

"Have you told either of them yet?" I asked.

"Not yet. I just found out," she cried.

"Well, you have to tell them so that they can get checked!" I insisted.

"I know. I will," she agreed.

"Well, in the meantime, I'm gonna make me a doctor's appointment to get checked to make sure that I'm good," Christine explained.

"Yeah, that's a good idea," I added.

CHAPTER 12

Make It

I'm filled with emotion and I just can't take it, but I believe in love, so we've gotta make it.

It would be a lie to say that I didn't want to be here, so I won't fake it.

I'm willing to do whatever it takes to make it.

Love is pure, love is kind, love is forgiving, love is sacred.

I believe in love, so we've gotta make it.

Sometimes, I feel all alone, and I wonder, Is life worth living? Why not forsake it?

But then, I think of you and know that life is priceless, so we've gotta make it.

Sometimes, life is too much; I just can't take it. I wanna throw in the towel and just forsake it because I no longer believe that love is sacred, but through it all, I'm glad we made it.

Senior year came and went faster than I could have ever imagined.

Somehow, by the grace of God, we all managed to graduate just like we began: together. Graduation was right around the corner and we all managed to put our differences to the side since Nicole's HIV scare. It turned out that Adrian was the one who gave it to Nikki, but because Christine had always had protected sex with him, she was not infected with the virus. Chrissy later gave us that information after she found out that her test results were negative. She was proud that she had always listened to her mother's lectures about using condoms no matter who she was sleeping with, especially if she wasn't married.

Christine and her mom always had an open line of communication, so things like sex were always up for discussion no matter what the circumstance was. Chris also got tested and his results have yet to be told because he left town faster than I could blink and we never heard from him again. Nikki was doing well and took each day one step at a time. Christine and Nicole's relationship hasn't been fully repaired, but they are diligently working on it, and that's all that matters. For the first time in a long time, we all finally began to see the bigger picture— the true meaning of friendship and how vital it is to the human soul.

Graduation day had finally arrived. Christine was Magna Cum Laude of our class so her parents flew their entire family into town to celebrate. Nicole's parents and siblings were all in attendance, and as for me, well, let's just say that my mother was there in spirit because once again, she was a no-show. Her absence was something that I had gotten used to over time, not that it hurt any less—I have just arrived at a place in my life where I now accept people for who they really are and love them as they are. Watching Nicole and Christine's excitement as their families arrived in town made me miss my little brother more than ever. I know that he is always smiling down on me and I know that he would have been proud of me; after all, I did this for myself and for him.

As I zipped my gown and positioned my cap on my head, I said one last prayer in remembrance of Anthony. I began to be filled with gratefulness for how far I've come, and most of all, for the love and loyalty of my friends.

The music began playing as we marched out with smiles, feeling proud of our accomplishments. Christine's speech was filled with motivation, perseverance, and faith. The crowd gave her a standing ovation when she finished.

Finally, the moment had arrived for us to cross the stage.

My heart dropped into my stomach as I stood. As I carefully tiptoed across the stage and tried not to fall flat on my face in the six-inch heels that I chose to wear, I could see a frail woman standing beside the stage. She held a disposable Kodak camera in her hand and was waiting for me to complete my walk after shaking the chancellor's hand. To my surprise, that frail woman was my mother! I had never been so elated in my life! I didn't care how she had gotten here or who she came with; all that mattered to me was that she was there to witness my accomplishment and celebrate with me.

As I exited the stage and headed to take my seat, I happily waved to let her know that I saw her and blew a kiss to show my gratitude for her being there.

As soon as graduation was over, I ran to find my mother to give her the biggest hug that I had ever given anyone. I was overjoyed that I finally had someone who I could call family there with me alongside all of my friends and their families. Nothing else in the world mattered to me in that moment. I eagerly introduced my mom to Nicole's parents and Christine's parents.

Soon after graduation was over, Christine's parents invited everyone out to Rosewood's Mansion at Turtle Creek, where they had made reservations at a restaurant that was well-known for its fine dining in Dallas. We laughed all night long together and enjoyed each other's company. Nothing was more monumental to me than this very moment.

About the Author:

Nadine A. Goins is a native of Milwaukee, WI, by way of Atlanta, GA. She graduated with a bachelor of science degree in Business Administration and Management from the University of Arkansas at Pine Bluff. She enjoys feeding the homeless in the city of Atlanta, as well as donating clothes and shoes to battered women and children in need at the local Safe Haven. She hopes that her initiative to do good in the community sparks the actions of others to do the same in their communities also. She aspires to be a motivational speaker to the youth and hopes that the message in this book will spark conversations about the importance of safe sex nationwide, for she believes that children are indeed our future and our responsibility to support as a whole.

Synopsis:

Destiny is a millennial kid who grew up in the heart of Memphis, Tennessee, whose mother struggled with addiction her entire life. Destiny is determined to beat the odds and get a college education despite the lack of family support. When she arrives at college, she meets two girls by the names of Nicole and Christine. All three ladies come from different walks of life, but they all have one thing in common: FAITH. While navigating their college lives together, the ladies develop an unbreakable bond that is nearly shattered with tragic loss on every end. Somehow, they manage to graduate college at the same time, but will their friendship be enough to survive the turmoil that they're faced with?

www.ingramcontent.com/pod-product-compliance
Lightning Source LLC
Chambersburg PA
CBHW071354170626
46811CB00003B/1131